**Placing a hand on either side of her head, he drew back and gazed down at her.**

He ran his thumb lightly along the fading bruise on her cheek, and she blinked and stared up at him. Her eyes were so dark. They absorbed the light like black velvet. He kissed the corners of her eyelids where tears still clung and he tasted salt.

"We should——" he started, but a loud metallic screech drowned out his words. Without stopping to think, he grabbed Juliana and dove through the open closet door.

He twisted in midair, trying to take the brunt of the impact. His shoulder slammed against the floor.

A deafening crash shook the walls and sent splinters, debris and dust flying. Dawson hunched his shoulders and rolled, putting his back to the destruction. He wrapped his arms around her head and ducked his.

One slight move and she could have been killed. And he still hadn't told her who he really was.

# MALLORY KANE

## PRIVATE SECURITY

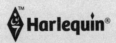

TORONTO  NEW YORK  LONDON
AMSTERDAM  PARIS  SYDNEY  HAMBURG
STOCKHOLM  ATHENS  TOKYO  MILAN  MADRID
PRAGUE  WARSAW  BUDAPEST  AUCKLAND

For Michael, with all my love

Recycling programs
for this product may
not exist in your area.

ISBN-13: 978-0-373-69618-5

PRIVATE SECURITY

Copyright © 2012 by Rickey R. Mallory

This edition published by arrangement with Harlequin Books S.A.

For questions and comments about the quality of this book please contact us at Customer_eCare@Harlequin.ca.

® and TM are trademarks of the publisher. Trademarks indicated with ® are registered in the United States Patent and Trademark Office, the Canadian Trade Marks Office and in other countries.

www.Harlequin.com

**Printed in U.S.A.**

# ABOUT THE AUTHOR

Mallory has two very good reasons for loving reading and writing. Her mother was a librarian, who taught her to love and respect books as a precious resource. Her father could hold listeners spellbound for hours with his stories. He was always her biggest fan.

She loves romance suspense with dangerous heroes and dauntless heroines, and enjoys tossing in a bit of her medical knowledge for an extra dose of intrigue. After twenty-five books published, Mallory is still amazed and thrilled that she actually gets to make up stories for a living.

Mallory lives in Tennessee with her computer-genius husband and three exceptionally intelligent cats. She enjoys hearing from readers. You can write her at mallory@mallorykane.com or via Harlequin Books.

## Books by Mallory Kane

*Ultimate Agents
**Black Hills Brotherhood
‡‡The Delancey Dynasty

# CAST OF CHARACTERS

**John Dawson**—The security and investigations specialist who no longer goes by the name Dawson Delancey, swears to prove who's responsible for six deaths in a casino's structural failure, even if it's his own dad. But how will he keep the brave, beautiful daughter of the casino manager who died that day from leaving his heart in ruins?

**Juliana Caprese**—This would-be private eye won't give up until the person responsible for her father's death is brought to justice. She believes in John Dawson, the sexy investigator who says he wants the same thing she does, until she finds out who he really is.

**Michael Delancey**—Dawson's father swears he didn't cause the collapse that killed six people at the Golden Galaxy Casino. But how far will he go to stay out of prison? As far as putting his own son's life in danger?

**Brian Hardy**—The police detective put Michael Delancey in prison once, when he worked in Vice. Now he's investigating the man again—this time for murder.

**Randall Knoblock**—This contractor who worked on the Golden Galaxy Casino is a hired gun who goes where the money is. But suddenly he's nowhere to be found. His testimony could free John's father, or convict him, if only John could track him down.

**Vittorio (Tito) Vega**—A prominent real-estate developer and patron of the arts, Vega has his hands in every profitable venture on the Gulf Coast. Is he the generous entrepreneur he appears to be, or does he harbor a vengeful secret?

# Chapter One

By the time the woman struggled out of the taxi, Dawson knew the color of her panties. They were *pink*.

He swallowed hard and lifted the binoculars to the blue sling that cradled her left arm and hindered her movements. What had happened to her? Three days ago on Monday, when he'd finally spotted her checking the post office box, she'd been fine.

She awkwardly tugged her skirt down, and he lowered the glasses. He hadn't had time to stare at her on Monday. Now he checked out the whole package.

Tall, lithe, knockout legs and finger-tangling black hair. When she bent to pull out three plastic grocery bags, he raised the glasses again. He adjusted the focus for an excellent view of her excellent backside.

Then he noticed something at her waist. Something that glinted in the afternoon sunlight. He adjusted the focus. Under the trim jacket she wore, tucked into her skirt, was a handgun. She was carrying.

"Damn," he muttered. Juliana Caprese was a dealer at the Black Jack Casino in Biloxi. What the hell was she doing with a gun? His gaze lit on the blue sling again. Maybe it had something to do with how she'd injured her arm.

He shrugged and laid the binoculars on the passenger seat beside him. Only one way to find out. He got out of the car and sauntered down the sidewalk, timing his approach so that he'd be in her way when she headed for the stairs to her apartment building.

She hooked all three grocery bags over her right wrist and dug into her jacket pocket. The bags swung back and forth, and even from his distance, Dawson could see the way the plastic handles bit into the skin of her forearm. She wasn't going to make it without dropping something. He sped up slightly.

Juliana Caprese grimaced as the plastic bags dug into her flesh. She fumbled for the bills she'd stuck in her pocket to give the taxi driver. With her left arm out of commission, even the smallest task was a pain. She finally snagged the bills with two fingers and tugged. As she did, she felt one of the plastic straps tear. Her arm jerked as the strap broke and a bag hit the sidewalk. She heard the unmistakable crunch of eggshells breaking.

"Damn it!" she snapped, glaring at the taxi driver, but her effort was wasted. He lounged complacently behind the wheel talking on his microphone in a language she couldn't place.

Before she could lift her right arm to hand the lazy thug his fare, a man stepped right in front of her.

Startled, her instinctive reaction was to run. The last time someone had taken her by surprise she'd ended up with a bruised face, a banged-up knee and a dislocated shoulder.

But there was nowhere for her to go. She was blocked in by the taxi, the man and the spilled groceries.

Then she saw what the man was doing. He thrust two twenties into the driver's face. "I've got your cab number," he said mildly. "Your boss will hear about your lazy butt."

The driver muttered something in a foreign language and sped away.

Juliana crouched to pick up her bag of broken eggs. The man crouched at the same time.

"I got it," he said.

She held out the crumpled bills. "Here."

But he snagged the bag and stood, leaving her at eye level with the front of his jeans.

*Oh, boy,* she thought, her mouth going dry. The sight of leanly muscled thighs straining against worn denim took her breath away. For an instant, she just stared.

"Need help?" he asked, a definite hint of amusement in his voice. He held out his hand.

She ignored it and rose, wincing when her knee threatened to buckle. "Take this," she snapped, thrusting the money toward him again.

But he didn't even look at it. "Let me help you with those," he said, deftly hooking a finger around the straining plastic straps on her wrist.

"No," she said immediately. "I'm fine."

But he already had them. Apprehension took hold of her again. "Please give me back my groceries."

"I don't think this bag qualifies as groceries any longer," he responded in that same amused voice. "I think your eggs have graduated from groceries to garbage."

Juliana bit her cheek to stop herself from chuckling. She raised her gaze to his and frowned at the look in his very bright blue eyes. He was watching her with a disturbing intensity. "I'll check them when I get upstairs," she said shortly, suddenly feeling vulnerable.

She glanced around. Where had he come from? When the taxi had stopped, there was no one on the street. She knew, because ever since she'd been attacked two days ago, she'd been hypervigilant. And she'd started carrying her gun. She was not about to be caught with no means of self-defense again. *Ever.*

The man's eyes narrowed and his brows lowered dangerously. "What happened to you?" he asked gruffly.

"What?"

"Your face. Your arm."

"Accident," she tossed out. "May I have my bags now?"

"You live here?"

He was starting to scare her. She backed away toward the steps to her building. She glared at him again, avoiding those laser eyes, looking at his mouth instead. But that turned out to be a mistake. His mouth was wide and straight, with a lower lip that she was sure would— *Stop it,* the little voice inside her head said. *You don't know where that mouth has been.*

She glanced over her shoulder and took another step backward. She was nearly at the steps to her building.

"Whoa, hang on," the man said quickly. "You're Juliana Caprese, right?"

Her heart lurched. He knew her name. She half turned, ready to run up the steps. She didn't need those groceries that badly.

"Wait, please. My name's Dawson," he offered. "I guess I'm not handling this well. I don't mean to frighten you. I just want to ask you a question or two. Did you get the business card I left at Kaplan Wright?"

That surprised her. So this was the John Dawson who'd left the card at the architect's office. She paused, but she moved her hand to her side, ready to grab her weapon.

"Hey, I'm not going to hurt you. Like I said, I just want to ask you some questions."

She narrowed her gaze. "Ask me some questions? Well, you're right. You aren't handling it well. Accosting me in the street is not a good way to start." She let her hand drift backward again, wondering how long it would take her to grab her gun.

*Too long,* the little voice answered.

"Ms. Caprese," he said quickly, "there's no reason for you to be afraid of me. I'm on your side."

"My side?" That shocked her. She clamped her jaw and lifted her chin. She didn't relax her hand. "My side of what?" she asked harshly.

"The collapse of the Sky Walk."

Her heart, already racing, took a header against her chest wall and stole her breath. She sucked in air greedily. Her heel hit the bottom step and she almost stumbled.

"Look Mr.—Dawson," she grated. "I'm—" What was she about to tell him? That she was armed? There was no way she could get her hand on her Smith & Wesson 3913 before he stopped her. He was six inches taller and outweighed her by at least seventy pounds. He could disarm her without breaking an egg, if there were any left whole.

Even so, she was curious. "What do you mean you're on my side?"

The man named John Dawson, whose card was sitting on her desk upstairs, gave her a hint of a smile. "I'm looking into the collapse of the Sky Walk, just like you. We could both benefit from working together."

"Are you a cop?" she snapped, just as the rest of the printing on the card rose in her mind. It said D&D Services, Inc. By Appointment Only.

He allowed his mouth to stretch into a smile that revealed an unexpected dimple in his cheek. "Nope. I'm just a private citizen, looking into this on my own, same as you, but I've got better equipment." He stopped and let his gaze drift over her.

"Well, some of it's better," he amended.

She bristled at the double entendre. She didn't like him. He was too cocky, too friendly—too good-looking. And she had the feeling he hadn't shown up here on a whim. He wasn't the type to act on impulse—his eyes were too sharp, too calculating. She was sure he'd learned everything he could about her before he'd ever decided to approach her.

"Why?" she asked.

"Why what?"

"Why are you interested in the Sky Walk?"

His smile didn't fade, but those blue eyes took on a smoky hue. He shook his head. "Let's just say I have a need to know what happened, too. Look, Juliana—may I call you Juliana?"

"No, you may not. I don't need any help. I'm doing just fine. Now please, give me my bags."

He held them out. One of them was dripping raw, slimy egg. She grabbed on to the straps, touching his hand. She jerked away, but not fast enough to miss that it was warm and large and strong, with long fingers and calluses on his palms. She peered up at his face. He had the looks and the build of an actor or a model, but his hands told her he'd done manual labor. Interesting.

No. No. *No. Not* interesting. "I have to go. I'm not interested in working with you—or anyone else," she said frostily. She started toward the steps to her apartment building, then looked back.

"Thank you for—" She lifted the hand carrying the bags. As she started to climb the first step, he spoke.

"Juliana, who attacked you?"

She whirled. His brows were lowered again in that dangerous expression. She pressed her lips together. For an instant, she felt an overwhelming urge to tell him what had happened. With that fierce glare and those strong, beautiful workman's hands, he could keep her safe from all harm. She was sure of that.

But what if he was lying? What if he worked for the people

who wanted to stop her from looking into her father's death? The people who'd attacked her?

She turned back to the stairs and felt raw egg dripping onto her foot.

DAWSON WAS READY TO GIVE UP—at least for the moment. He stole one more look at her excellent backside and saw her knee give way. She cried out and grabbed for the stair rail. The grocery bags hit the steps and a bag of salad, two cartons of yogurt, a bottle of milk and the last two unbroken eggs went flying.

He dived and managed to catch her before she hit the steps.

They tumbled down the two steps to the sidewalk, him doing his best to break her fall. He landed on his elbow and it screamed with very unfunny pain.

He set her away from him, but not before he got a whiff of fresh, clean, peppermint-scented hair and a demonstration of how fit she was. Her bottom was not just shapely, but it was also firm and toned.

"Hey, Juliana, you all right?" he asked, setting her off him and rising to a crouch beside her, feeling a slimy wetness seeping through the knee of his pants. *Egg.* Damn it.

In answer, she rolled over onto her knees and used one hand to push herself to her feet. Once she was upright, she took her weight off her right knee and a wince crossed her face.

He stood, too, and looked down at the front of her skirt. It had ridden five inches up her thighs, proving that her legs were knockouts. Pink yogurt had spilled down its front and was sliding down her right leg toward the egg yolk.

"Argh!" she growled and tugged at the hem, then glared at him as if it all was his fault.

He spread his hands. "Sorry—" he drawled.

"Don't—" She took a deep breath. "Just don't!" She turned

carefully and started up the stairs. She was favoring her right knee and each time she put her weight on it, she smothered a groan.

"Hey, wait," he said. "You hurt your knee."

She kept going.

"Jules—" He started to grab her arm and stop her, but then he thought better of it. Instead, he picked up a plastic bag and loaded the few intact groceries into it. The eggs were dead, as was the yogurt. But the bag of salad was fine, the quart of milk seemed okay and the French baguette was still whole. He picked up a bunch of asparagus and a package of gnocchi. Then he vaulted up the stairs and stood on the second-floor landing, trying to remember what her apartment number was.

He didn't have to wonder long. A mild curse in a feminine voice came from apartment three.

He knocked on the door. "Jules? I've got your groceries."

After a couple of minutes, the door opened. That haughty glare was in place, and there were tears on her cheeks. She held a wet cloth in her hand and the yogurt on the front of her skirt was smeared.

He held up the bag. "I saved what I could."

She reached for the bag, but he held it out of reach. "Invite me in. I need to wash my hands."

She leaned against the door and shook her head. "I don't know who you are or why you're stalking me, but if you don't leave right now, I'm going to call the police."

"I'm not stalking you. I rescued your butt *and* saved your groceries. Now we can leave the door open, or we can talk outside or I'll buy you a cup of coffee—"

At that she gave him a disgusted look and gestured toward her stained skirt and her yogurt-and-egg-streaked legs.

"Okay. I can wait out here until you clean up, but I'm warning you, I won't leave until we talk. I can promise you that you will thank me afterward."

Her brows rose. "I sincerely doubt that."

He stepped to the side of the door and slid down the wall to a crouch, his forearms resting on his knees.

"Are you kidding me?" she blurted.

Dawson glanced up at her sidelong. "Nope."

"What's your interest in the Sky Walk?" she asked suspiciously.

"I'll tell you," he said, rising, "if you'll invite me in." He waggled his eyebrows. "You know you want to."

She immediately reached behind her for the door handle, so he stopped, his hand up. "Okay. Jules—Ms. Caprese—you want to know who was responsible for your father's death. I want to know the same thing. I have resources that you can't possibly have. Plus I have experience in surveillance. I want to help you."

She stared at him for a long moment. She shrugged, then winced. "I don't—" She stopped. She looked behind her, then back at him, frowning. "You have experience in surveillance?" she asked.

He nodded.

After a few seconds, she inclined her head, begrudgingly inviting him inside.

Her apartment looked like her—trim and elegant and decked out in black and white. The walls were brilliant white. The couch was black and white striped and flanked by a white club chair with large black flowers. The only color was the red rug on the floor and the bookcase, which bulged with hardbacks and paperbacks.

Juliana couldn't believe her eyes. As soon as he stepped through the door, her small apartment changed. She'd decorated it to be elegant and sophisticated. But with him standing there, it suddenly seemed kind of prissy. She closed the door behind him but didn't lock it. "Who *are* you?" she asked.

He reached into his shirt pocket and pulled out a card. He glanced at it, his mouth set, before handing it to her.

Juliana took the card reluctantly by its edge. She didn't want to risk touching him again. It read D&D Services, Inc., Biloxi, Mississippi. John Dawson. It was a duplicate of the one sitting on her desk. There was no street address. Just a phone number and the words *By appointment only.*

She looked up at him, searching his face. "John Dawson," she said, trying out the name.

He raised a brow. "Yep."

*John Dawson.* An average, run-of-the-mill name for a man who was anything but.

"Okay, Mr. Dawson." She took a deep breath. "You didn't seek me out just so you could help me. What's your game? And how do I know you're not working for the same people who—" She stopped and pressed her lips together.

"Who what?" he said sharply. "Did that to you?" He pointed to her shoulder and then to the scrape on her cheek. "What happened?"

Juliana turned away, trying to figure out why she had such an urge to confide in this stranger. The little voice in the back of her mind that had protected her many times spoke up.

*Are we sure we can trust this Dawson? We don't know anything about him except what he's told us. For all we know he could be the person behind your attack.*

## Chapter Two

To give herself a little space, Juliana walked over to her refrigerator and filled a glass of water. She took a couple of sips, then turned around.

"Would you like some water?" she asked. Only a few feet separated them. And that wasn't nearly enough. He filled up her little apartment with his tall, lanky frame. She'd already been introduced, intimately, to his long legs and lean, powerful thighs and the fact that he was definitely a virile, heterosexual male when she'd fallen on him. Add to that his broad, sinewy shoulders and those really beautiful hands, and the sum was a seriously hot guy.

But there was no way she trusted him. He'd shown up like a good Samaritan just as she dropped her groceries. But unlike a helpful passerby, he knew her name. Had he been following her? Worse, had he been waiting for a chance to worm his way into her apartment?

Suddenly, it didn't matter how hot he was. He was a stranger—a stranger who knew an awful lot about her. Her gaze snapped to her front door.

*Big mistake, letting him get between us and the door,* her little voice chided her. *We'll never make it before he catches us.*

He looked at her, glanced over his shoulder at the door, then back at her. "Come on. If you're not going to trust me, then I probably should leave. But I'm betting that together we can figure out what happened at the Golden Galaxy Casino and put the person responsible for the Sky Walk's collapse behind bars. I'm not sure either of us can do it alone." He sighed. "So what do you say?"

She leveled a suspicious gaze at him. "How do you know my name?" she asked.

"Because you put an ad in the paper looking for information about the collapse of the Sky Walk."

She set her jaw and shook her head. "My name wasn't on the ad."

"No, it wasn't. I found the post office box and watched it. When you showed up to check it, I got your license plate."

She gasped, trepidation tightening her chest. "You've been following me," she accused, but then a different emotion blossomed in her chest. "Wait a minute, if you were there…did you…did you see who attacked me and stole my letter?"

Dawson frowned. "That's what happened? Someone stole a letter you got through the ad? I can't say I'm surprised. Didn't you realize putting that ad in the paper made you a sitting duck? You're lucky all you've got were a few bruises."

She flushed.

"It didn't take me any time to find you." He'd hung around the post office box for a couple of days, long enough to spot her checking the box. Then he'd had his brother Reilly, a cop for the Chef Voleur Sheriff's Office, run her plates.

Juliana Caprese, the daughter of the casino manager who was killed when the famous Sky Walk at the Golden Galaxy Casino collapsed three months ago, owned the car. That surprised and intrigued him.

"When did it happen?"

"Two days ago—Tuesday. It was a small man in a hoodie. I'd just taken the letter out of the box. It was the first response I'd gotten to the ad. As soon as I walked outside, he knocked me down and grabbed it. That's when—" She gestured toward her shoulder.

"And that bruise on the side of your face?"

"Where he hit me."

"Bastard," Dawson said, not even trying to mask his fury at the scumbag. "Who sent the letter?"

"I didn't open it. It was addressed to the post office box and there was no return address."

"What about the postmark?"

"I didn't look at it that closely. I was late for work. I was going to open it on my break." She made a face. "I should have opened it. There was something inside."

"What do you mean? Something besides paper?"

"It was a regular number 10 envelope, the kind you pay bills in. But there was something besides paper inside it. About two inches long. Kind of flat."

"You couldn't tell what it was? What it felt like?"

"No, I was in a hurry."

"And that's the only response you've gotten?"

"I haven't been back." She indicated her shoulder. "It's a little hard to get around."

"What about the man who attacked you? Did you get a look at his face? Any identifying marks?"

"Yes, he had tattoos on his arms—" She touched her forearm just above her wrist. "At least that far, which was all I saw. Everything happened so fast. But they were colorful."

"What did the police say?"

Juliana's front teeth scraped her lower lip. She looked away. "I didn't call the police."

Dawson's fury morphed into irritation at her. "Why the hell not? Because you decided you'd handle this vigilante-style? Or because you don't have a carry permit for that Ladysmith you've got in your waistband?"

She looked surprised and guilty. "I'm no vigilante, but I did decide I wasn't going to be attacked again."

"Good for you. Question is, do you know how to use that weapon? Because if you don't—"

She nodded. "My dad taught me." Her mouth twisted. "He thought I should be prepared."

Dawson sat back. "Are you any good?"

Her eyes snapped. "You want to go to the pistol range and check me out?"

He shook his head. "I'll wait until your shoulder gets better. Wouldn't want you claiming a handicap." He regarded her solemnly. "Why did you put the ad in the paper?"

Her chin went up. "Because someone out there knows what happened to the Sky Walk."

"You're looking for someone to blame for your father's death."

"No, that's not it, Mr. Dawson," she said.

He held up a hand. "Hey, just Dawson, okay?"

"Fine. Dawson. I'm not looking for someone to blame. I *know* who's to blame. I just need evidence to prove it."

Dawson's eyes narrowed. "You *know?* Who? Who do you *know* caused your father's death?"

"Michael Delancey, the contractor who built the Golden Galaxy. I've talked to the detectives, the crime scene investigators, Mr. Kaplan, the architect who drew up the plans— they all believe that something must have been wrong with the metal framework. Whether it was substandard materials or shoddy workmanship they don't know. But although Mr. Kaplan told me the materials list was marginally up to code, there were definite shortcuts taken. That's what happens when a contractor cuts costs to make a bigger profit."

Dawson kept his expression and his voice even. "From what I hear, the Delanceys are loaded. Why would he bother?"

"Maybe he's in money trouble. Maybe he just wasn't concerned. I don't care why he did it. I just care about getting justice for my dad. He didn't deserve to die like that."

Dawson nodded grimly. "I'm interested in what happened to the Sky Walk, too. For a client who was injured."

Juliana's brows rose. "A client? Who?" Her gaze narrowed. "Just what is D&D Services? Your card is pretty snobbish, with no indication of what your services are."

"I figure if someone needs my services, they'll know."

"Well, assume I don't."

"I own a security agency. I provide bodyguards, security systems, investigative services. My motto is Dedication and Discretion." He made a little gesture. "*D* and *D*."

She gasped, then her eyes widened and to his surprise, her mouth widened in a grin. "You're a private eye?" she asked.

He frowned at her. What the hell was so funny? "Yep, you could say that."

"A *real* private investigator! Wow!" Her dark eyes snapped with interest. "*I'm* going to be a private investigator."

Okay. That shocked him. "You're what?"

"I've always wanted to be a private eye. I got my degree in Administrative Justice. But I can't afford to start my own business, and nobody wants to hire someone with no experience."

"So you're working as a dealer in a casino."

She studied him for a few seconds. "I need to know who your client is."

"Look, Jules—"

Her jaw set again. "Don't call me that. My name is Juliana."

"Fine. Juliana. I have a contractual obligation to my client. I can't tell you anything."

She shook her head. "I see what this is about. You don't want to *work* with me. You just want to get your hands on what I've found out, so you don't have to reinvent the wheel."

She waved a hand. "Just how long have you been following me? Quite a while, I'd guess, because you figured out that I would be going to visit Kaplan Wright Architects, and left your card there. Pretty good detective work. But no, I have no reason to work with you. It could have been your client who stole my letter."

Then a harsh laugh escaped her lips. "You could be working for Michael Delancey, for all I know."

Dawson fought to keep his face from showing any reaction. "I guarantee you I'm interested in the same thing you are."

"Yeah? What thing?"

"Getting to the truth. What's your thing?"

"I told you. I want to know who was behind the collapse of the Sky Walk."

"Didn't you just say you know who it was? Michael Delancey."

Her gaze wavered. "I think it's him. He was the contractor after all, but I need to be sure." She paused. "What about you? Do you think it was Michael Delancey?"

Dawson didn't trust his ability to hold on to his placid expression, so he stood and walked over to the window. "I don't know whose fault it was, but I can tell you this. I will do everything I can to get to the truth."

"No matter who it hurts?" she persisted.

He thought about Michael Delancey, the heir to a vast fortune and a tainted legacy. Infamous Senator Con Delancey's son. Michael had gone into construction rather than pursue politics, wanting to distance himself from his scandalous father.

Once his firstborn son was old enough, he'd brought him into the business. But the son soon grew suspicious of his father's business practices. Then when Michael was indicted for gross negligence and gross misconduct, his son had separated himself from his father. He'd quit the construction business and started his own company.

*No matter who it hurts?* Juliana Caprese had asked Dawson.

If he pursued the truth, he wouldn't stop until he'd found it. And if the truth led him to Michael Delancey's door, then so be it.

"No matter who it hurts," John Dawson Delancey answered.

At that instant his phone rang. He fished it out of the holder at his belt and checked the display.

*Speak of the devil.* He grimaced as he killed the connection. "That's a call I've been expecting," he told Juliana. "I have to go. I'll call you later."

"But you don't have my phone—" She stopped when he sent her an amused glance. "Oh." Her eyes sparked with interest. "You used your private eye tricks to get my number, didn't you?"

He shook his head tiredly. But as he headed for the door, she called after him, "You have *got* to tell me how you did that."

He grinned to himself as an image rose in his mind of a gorgeous, long-legged private eye with her left arm in a sling, her right hand brandishing a weapon and her skirt blowing up to reveal pink panties. It would be very interesting to see if Juliana Caprese became a private investigator. Only trouble was, eventually she'd figure out who he was, and once she did, the only thing he'd see of her was that firm butt disappearing from his life. But for now he could enjoy his image of her as a gumshoe. Did they make high-heeled gumshoes?

Dawson climbed into his nondescript Honda Accord and set the phone down in the console. He didn't like driving the boring silver mom car, although it handled well. He much preferred driving his new Corvette, but the Accord was perfect for tailing or surveillance. Its greatest attribute was that it looked like any other car on the street.

As he pulled away from the curb he frowned. He had to call his father back. He hit Redial and listened to the phone ring on his Bluetooth connection. The name on the display read Michael Delancey. He'd removed the word *Dad* years ago.

"Yel-lo." The familiar voice pricked Dawson's chest like a thorn. His dad had finally come out of his melancholy and started answering the phone. For months after he was released from prison, he'd sat in front of the TV, not speaking unless he was forced to.

"It's me," Dawson said shortly. "You called?"

"Hey, son. I was just checking to see if you had any news."

Dawson grimaced. He didn't want Michael Delancey to call him son. "No. I told you, I'd call you when I found out anything. I warned you not to call my cell phone. It's for work only. Leave me a message at my condo or I swear I'll get my number changed."

"Okay. No problem." Michael's voice was almost toneless. Dawson knew he wasn't really listening to him.

"I mean it!" he snapped.

"I get it!" Michael snapped back and Dawson knew he did. "What about that ad? Did you track down who placed it?"

"I'm working on that." He wasn't about to tell his dad that it was Vincent Caprese's daughter who'd offered ten thousand dollars for the name of the person responsible for the Sky Walk's collapse.

"You've been working on it for weeks. Damn it, Dawson, the police have already questioned me three times. I can't go back to prison. I can't!"

"Why do you think they keep coming back? Obviously they don't like something you're telling them. Why don't you give them the straight story for once?" Dawson turned into the parking lot of his waterfront condo overlooking Biloxi's Back Bay.

There was a pause on the other end of the line. "You still think I'm not? Damn it to hell, if I had anything else that would help—" He broke off with a frustrated huff.

There was no mistaking the desperation in his father's voice. Dawson steeled himself against the compassion that he felt rising in his chest—compassion his dad didn't deserve.

"Dawson? You've got to believe me. I didn't have anything to do with the Sky Walk's collapse. If my own son won't believe me, I guess I'm sunk."

The Sky Walk had been a multimillion-dollar two-level suspended walkway that stretched above the main floor of the Golden Galaxy Casino in Waveland, Mississippi, the newest and largest casino on the Mississippi Gulf Coast.

"I've got to go."

"Okay, son. Call your mother later. She's taking a nap now."

Dawson disconnected and looked at his watch. It was three o'clock in the afternoon. His lips thinned. *Taking a nap* was family code for at least one bottle of wine down the chute, if not two. He sighed.

It was hell being the oldest kid—oldest son, he amended. If his sister Rosemary had lived, she'd be thirty-four, two years older than he. But she'd been murdered twelve years before, so she would always be twenty-two.

The twins were older than that now. At the thought of Ryker and Reilly, his identical younger brothers, he gave a gruff snort. They'd gone completely bonkers over the past year—not even thirty and married within six months of each other—right on the heels of a notorious serial-killer case in St. Tammany Parish in Louisiana.

Ryker had married the only woman who'd survived Albert

Moser's obsessive killing spree, and Reilly had married the serial killer's daughter.

Dawson shook his head. He was five years older than them, and he didn't even live in the same hemisphere as marriage. It would be a cold day in hell when he fell into that trap.

It was bizarre. They'd grown up in the same family. As Dawson liked to say, they put the funk in dysfunctional.

Rosemary's death, or to be precise, her disappearance, had begun their mother's fall into discreet, genteel alcoholism. Then, eight years ago, Michael Delancey had gone to prison, his mother had gone into the bottle and Dawson had separated himself from anything having to do with his father.

Inside his condo he tossed keys and jacket onto the kitchen table and laid his shoulder holster beside them. Then he headed for the shower.

As he dropped his egg-and-yogurt-stained shirt and pants into the hamper and stepped under the hot spray, a vision rose in his brain. Juliana Caprese, private eye, with a pink sling to match her pink panties and brandishing a big gun.

Immediately, insistently, something else rose, as well. His buttocks and thighs tightened as the shower's spray changed to caressing fingers. He groaned and raised his face to the hot water, enjoying the feel of it streaming down his neck, across his sensitized nipples, over his abs and down, tickling across the sensitive skin just above his pubis.

He shuddered and contemplated turning off the hot water, but it was way too late for that, so he gave himself up to the fantasy of Juliana Caprese handling *his* weapon.

## Chapter Three

Juliana snuggled down under the fake fur throw and wriggled her toes inside her bunny slippers. The slippers didn't have bunny faces on them; they looked like the fluffy fat slippers that Bugs wore when he was relaxing.

On her lap was a stack of building permits, code inspections, material specifications, everything she'd been able to find in public records about the Golden Galaxy Casino. But on her mind was John Dawson.

After he'd left abruptly this afternoon, she'd looked up his website and called every government agency she could think of that might have information—good or bad—about D&D Services, Inc.

There was nothing out there about the company. Apparently what Dawson had told her was true. If people needed his services, they found him.

She remembered what else he'd said. *Dedication and discretion.* She had to hand it to him. He had the *discretion* part down pat. Every search had come up zero. No client list, no reviews, no referrals, no recommendations. Nor had she found anyone who *knew* anyone he'd worked for. In fact, although he had a website, it had hardly more information than his card. Not even the Better Business Bureau or the Attorney General's office had anything on D&D Services. The person she'd talked with at the Attorney General's office told her that no complaints had been filed against the company.

She'd also searched online for a John Dawson. There were dozens of Dawsons in Biloxi, and several John Dawsons. Once the entire Gulf Coast was included, she was looking at scores of possibilities. None of the phone numbers matched, though.

Juliana sighed and picked up her glass of wine. She took a sip, then realized she couldn't open a folder while holding the glass.

She was so sick of trying to do things with one arm. She slipped her left arm out of the sling. It hadn't been broken, just dislocated. The doctor had told her on Tuesday that after a couple of days she could start using it. That was today.

She transferred her wine to her left hand and lifted it to her lips, feeling a pop and a twinge that almost made her drop the glass. The doctor had told her the joint would probably pop for several months. He hadn't told her it would hurt. Still, she got the glass to her lips without spilling any.

Okay. That simplified things. She flipped through the folders in her lap with her right hand. She wanted to look at the note she'd found in her dad's things.

She found the file, neatly labeled in her father's precise hand. Golden Galaxy, Misc. Her heart squeezed, just like it did every time she saw his writing. She opened the folder and took out the plastic bag in which she'd placed a folded piece of lined paper. Inside the baggie, written in deliberate block letters, was the most damning piece of information she had about the construction failure that had killed her father and five other people.

Why hadn't her dad done something? Told somebody? Had the Sky Walk checked? He might be alive today.

She ran her fingers across the baggie, tracing the words.

BE CAREFUL, CAPRESE. THE SKY WALK'S DANGEROUS.
DELANCEY SHOULD KNOW. LOOK AT VEGA. HE HOLDS
GRUDGES.

There was no signature. Judging by the questions the
police had asked her, she was sure her dad hadn't shown it
to anyone. The police obviously didn't know about it.

She sure wasn't going to turn it over to them. They had
done absolutely nothing about arresting the man responsible for her dad's death. She wasn't letting anybody get their
hands on the note, not until she'd done everything she could
to identify the sender and find out what he knew about her
father's death.

The best clue she had was the name Vega. Compared to
her search for D&D Services and John Dawson, finding information about Vega had been a walk in the park. In the
Mississippi Gulf Coast area, Vittorio "Tito" Vega was a land-
mark. She found numerous newspaper articles touting his pa-
tronage of the arts and his civic involvement. But there were
also op-ed pieces that suggested that he had more money than
his real-estate investment business could account for, and that
he was rumored to be involved in loan-sharking and bribery.

The day after she'd found the note, she'd placed the ad.

Wanted: Information leading to the conviction of the
person(s) responsible for the collapse of the Sky Walk.
$10,000 reward. Respond to P.O. Box 7874.

She blew out a frustrated breath. She'd been so pleased
with herself, so cocky. Dawson was right. She might as well
have painted a bull's-eye on her back. All the guy who'd attacked her had to do was watch the post office box until she
received a reply, then snatch it.

*Like John Dawson.* A disturbing thought occurred to her.

He had admitted he'd watched the box. It could have been him who'd taken the letter. Not personally, she amended. The scumbag had been scrawny, dirty and covered with tattoos. Still, Dawson could have hired him.

She'd been on the verge of trusting the tall, hot private investigator. His assertion that he was working for someone who'd been injured in the Sky Walk's collapse had rung true.

But what if he was playing her? Whether he'd been responsible for stealing her letter, he wanted the information she had about the Sky Walk. And judging by his slick, flirty attitude and his shrewd blue eyes, he wouldn't balk at anything to get it.

DAWSON PUSHED HIS FINGERS through his damp hair and knocked on Juliana's door again. He was pretty sure she was home. After spilling her groceries and hurting her knee, he doubted she'd be going out on the town anytime soon. Besides, the single-serving packaged salad and the small baguette had hinted at a meal at home—for one.

He heard movement behind the door. He stepped back and positioned himself so his bland expression could be seen through the peephole.

He saw a shadow cover the minuscule window and heard a groan. "What do you want?" she called ungraciously.

He held the carton in his hand up to the peephole. "Brought you some eggs."

"Thank you," she called. "You can leave them by the door."

"Ah-ah-ah," he chided. "You don't get them until you let me in. I had to take care of some business earlier, but I still have questions."

"I guess you'll have to live without answers and I'll have to live without eggs." Her voice came through the door, tinged with a note of amusement.

"Have a heart, Caprese. I almost dropped them coming up the stairs. You know how that is."

The door opened slowly. She held out a hand.

"Sorry, you've got to let me in to get the eggs. Just a few minutes, two questions. That's all, I swear."

She shook her head. "Customer support is closed for the day."

Dawson quirked his mouth. "Cute. Now let me in. Like I told you, we can get a lot more done by working together."

"Right, you did say that. Why don't you make me a copy of what you have. I'll look at it and get back to you. You can give me your number—oh, wait. I already have it on your card." She moved to close the door, but he stuck his size-twelve Nike in the way.

She looked down, then back up, her eyes snapping. If they'd been dark lasers, he'd be neatly sliced in two lengthwise. "So that's how you want to play it," she commented. "Hold on a second while I get my gun."

He laughed. "That was your first mistake, rookie. You should have brought it with you."

She drew back, then showed her right hand again—holding the Ladysmith. "Like this?"

"Like that," he said. Neatly and lightning-quick, he caught her wrist, pressed a pressure point and took the gun away from her. He checked the safety. It was on.

"Don't play with firearms, little girl," he growled.

She frowned and her cheeks turned pink. "I wasn't really—"

He pushed past her and set her weapon on the coffee table. "That's the problem. Guns aren't something you fool around with. If you *weren't really,* then you shouldn't have brandished it."

She went around the coffee table and sat, quickly grabbing a folder that lay on the seat cushion beside her and stuffing it in between a stack of similar manila folders. Then she carefully slid her left arm into the sling that dangled from her shoulder and picked up a wineglass. She sipped nonchalantly.

Or tried to. But her cheeks were splotched with pink, and she refused to meet his gaze. She was obviously embarrassed about letting him take her gun.

"If you want to be a private eye," he said drily, "you'd better learn how to handle a gun."

"I know—"

"Don't ever—" he interrupted her "—hold your weapon at arm's length when your target is close enough to grab it." He set the eggs down on the coffee table and picked up her Ladysmith.

He demonstrated. "Stay far enough back that he can't reach it. If you're cornered and you can't step back, hold your weapon close and your arm closer. Press your elbow against your body. It gives you stability. Most importantly, never hold the gun with just one hand, and always check your balance. If the other person gains an advantage over you, you're dead."

She nodded carefully. "Got it," she said solemnly.

"Have you eaten?"

"What?" His abrupt change of subject took her aback.

"Eaten. You know, dinner?"

"I—"

"Great. I know you've got salad and bread. Let's have an omelet."

"I don't—"

But he'd already grabbed the carton of eggs and headed into the kitchen. Checking the refrigerator, he found some Swiss cheese, an open package of cooked bacon, the salad greens and a half-empty bottle of Cardini's Caesar salad dressing. "That should be enough for the two of us."

She craned her neck to look at him over her shoulder. "What are you doing?"

"I assume you like Caesar dressing. I'll just heat the bread, okay?"

"I don't— You don't—"

Dawson turned his back on her, smiling to himself. He had to admit it was fun keeping her off guard. He turned on the oven to preheat for the French bread, then he sniffed the packaged salad. He hated prepackaged greens, but these at least looked fresh. He emptied them into a glass bowl from her cupboard and ran water on them.

"What are you doing?" Her voice surprised him. She'd come into the kitchen under cover of the running water and was peering around him at the sink.

"Rinsing the greens," he said, trying his best to sound calm, although the peppermint scent of her hair brought to mind the erotic pressure of her firm bottom against him when he broke her fall earlier.

"But they're prerinsed."

"Trust me, rookie. Rinsing takes the plastic taste away. It'll be a hundred percent better." He held up a leaf of arugula. "Taste."

She looked up at him, her eyes smoky and filled with doubt, then opened her mouth.

When Juliana's lips parted, Dawson completely forgot about the arugula. His gaze slid along the soft, pink opening of her lips the way his tongue wanted to. His mouth watered at the imagined taste of her lips.

She looked up at him. Her gaze slid down to his neck when he swallowed, then drifted upward again and stopped at his mouth. She rose on tiptoe and leaned toward him.

Just when he'd decided to meet her halfway for a deep, delicious kiss, she plucked the leaf from his fingers and popped it into her mouth.

Then she licked her lips and lifted her chin. If he were a

betting man, he'd bet that she was laughing at him behind those eyes. "Mmm," she drawled. "Good."

It was his turn to be caught off guard. He was left aching with desire and curiosity when she turned on her heel and went back to the couch. What would she have done if he had kissed her?

Most likely thrown him out. He could have lost his best bet for finding out what she knew about the Sky Walk's collapse. He had to be careful. He hadn't met a woman in a long time who interested him as much as Juliana Caprese did. And because he only went to bed with women who interested him beyond the physical, that long time had long since become a very long time.

He broke the eggs into a bowl and added crumbled bacon. He couldn't find a cheese grater, so he chopped the cheese into chunks and tossed it in, then beat the eggs and poured the whole concoction into a heated pan.

But this wasn't even marginally about sex. It couldn't be, even though Juliana Caprese might be the most interesting woman he had ever met. He was here for one reason and one reason only. To find out what she knew about the collapse of the Sky Walk. He needed to know if her father's death was his father's fault.

The odor of toasty French bread filled his nostrils and made him realize he was staring at her black, tumbling hair. He opened the wall oven and grabbed the bread with his bare fingers, then dropped it onto the granite countertop. "Ouch," he muttered.

"Burn yourself?" Juliana asked cheerily, rising.

"Nope. Dinner's ready." He grabbed a plate and slid it under the loaf of bread, then carried it to the kitchen table.

"Burned French bread and watery salad. My favorite," Juliana said, going to the refrigerator and taking out a new bottle of white wine.

Dawson opened a couple of drawers until he found freshly washed dish towels. "Watch this," he said. He unfolded a towel and dumped the greens onto it. Then he caught the corners together and twirled the bundle a few times. When he folded the now-wet towel's corners back, the greens were dry and fresh-looking.

"Impressive," she said. She tucked the wine bottle under her left arm and began to twist the cap with her right hand.

He checked the omelet, flipped it and let it cook on the other side for about a minute. Then he cut it in two and slid the larger portion onto his plate and the smaller one onto hers.

Dinner was ready, but Juliana was still struggling with the bottle. Dawson sat down and crossed his arms, curious about how long it would take her to admit that she couldn't open the wine.

He was beginning to think she might have a stubborn streak.

She took the bottle from under her arm and stuck it between her knees. That didn't work any better. She muttered a colorful curse under her breath.

He chuckled. "Come on, rookie, let me open it for you. How'd you get the first bottle open?"

She sent him a withering look. "It was already open when—" She gingerly shrugged her left shoulder.

"So if I wasn't here, they'd find your skeleton in that chair, with the still-unopened wine bottle clutched in your bony fingers?"

Her mouth twitched. "I'll get it open eventually," she said flatly.

He plucked the bottle from between her knees and gave the cap a quick twist. Then he filled her glass. "Mind if I have some?"

"After all that work you did to open it? You deserve it."

Dawson tore the bread into small pieces so she wouldn't have to struggle with it, and then dug into his salad.

"Rinsing the salad did take the plasticky taste away," she said grudgingly.

He didn't bother answering. He was examining his reaction to sitting in her apartment breaking bread with her. It was a disturbing sensation. After a few minutes of silence, he realized that his discomfort was emanating from her. Despite their outwardly friendly banter, when she thought he wasn't looking, she eyed him with a guarded suspicion.

He finished his salad and dug into the omelet, watching her as he ate. She did pretty well with one arm. She'd take a bite of salad, then a bite of omelet, and set her fork down. She'd pick up a small piece of bread and slide it across the pat of butter on her plate and pop it into her mouth, take a sip of wine, then repeat the process.

He refilled their glasses, buttered another piece of bread and sat back, staring at her. "Your arm's not broken," he said.

She shook her head and considered him narrowly. "Just dislocated. I fell on it when he pushed me down."

"You didn't recognize him?"

"No. Are you relieved?"

Dawson frowned. "What's that supposed to mean?" he snapped.

She raised her brows and shrugged. "You tell me. You already admitted you were following me and watching the post office. Maybe you had someone else watching me, too."

"Come on, rookie," he growled, irritated. "I told you, we're on the same side."

"Yeah, maybe, until you get the information you want from me. You asked me what was in the letter I got. Are you sure you don't already have the answer to that question?"

Dawson stood so abruptly that he almost turned over his chair. He grabbed his plate and hers and tossed them into the sink with a clatter, then he jerked the salad and dressing off the table. In less than a minute he had the food put away. Then he turned on her, his face dark as a storm.

"You're accusing *me* of roughing you up and stealing your damn letter?" he roared, his words splitting the air like a thunderclap.

## Chapter Four

Juliana jumped when Dawson yelled at her. Although she should have expected it given the way he'd thrown her dishes around. Then the absurdity hit her.

She chuckled. "Did you seriously just bus the table before stopping to yell at me?" she asked.

Dawson scowled, then looked down at his hands. He still held the dishrag he'd used to wipe the table. He balled it up and fired a line drive into the sink, then scrubbed a palm across his evening stubble. "Chalk it up to a very dysfunctional childhood." He sighed.

He sounded sincere. Juliana resented him for making her want to believe him.

"If you want to be a private eye, you're going to have to get a hell of a lot better at reading people. Because trust me, rookie," Dawson said, fishing the dishrag out of the sink and folding it, "if I had that letter, I'm pretty sure I wouldn't be here begging you for information."

"I thought you told me you had info for me, too," she said, deciding for the moment to trust him.

*No,* not trust. But she would give him the benefit of the doubt for long enough to find out what he knew.

Then she'd see.

"Well, thank you for fixing dinner and cleaning up the

kitchen," she said, picking up her wineglass and heading back to the couch. She beat him by about two and a half seconds.

She slipped her arm out of the sling and grabbed the stack of folders as she sat. Her left shoulder protested, but at least her research was in her hands and not his.

He sat down beside her. "I see your shoulder's better," he said.

"A little. The doctor told me to keep it immobile and put ice on it for a couple of days, then I could start using it. If I don't move it too far or too fast, it's bearable."

"So what have you got in your lap there, rookie?"

She pressed her right hand down on the top folder as he casually reached for it. "Nothing you get to see until you share with me what you know. And—" she arched a brow at him "—it has to be something I don't already have."

"You don't already know this," he said confidently. He'd gotten it from Reilly, who'd pulled the info from the case files.

She turned toward him. "I guess we'll know soon. So what is it?"

"The initial report from the forensic engineer is that the Sky Walk looked just fine. No code violations, no recorded changes in materials from the submitted plans."

Juliana looked as if he'd slapped her. For a moment she just stared at him. "That can't be true," she finally said, shaking her head. "Mr. Kaplan, the architect, said—"

Dawson shrugged.

"No," Juliana snapped. "Whoever told you that was wrong."

"Sorry. This came from police records."

"But it—" She took a shaky breath. "It couldn't have just *broken*. There had to be something wrong with it. Things don't just break." Her eyes glittered with tears and her hands fisted around the top two manila folders on her lap.

Dawson felt a tug inside him, an urge to give her what she wanted so badly—someone to blame for her father's death. She might say she wanted the truth, might even believe it. But her search was for explanations, not facts. He only had a tiny scrap of hope to give her, but he offered it for what it was worth.

"It's a preliminary finding. But according to my source, the final report won't be ready for at least thirty days." He paused, then said, "Maybe then—"

"Not maybe. There *was* something wrong with the Sky Walk," she said again. "There was." Her fingers were squeezing the folders so tightly that their tips were turning bluish-white.

"Hey," he said, touching her hand. "Relax. If there's something wrong with the materials, the forensic engineer will find it."

She shook her head. "Michael Delancey has plenty of money. He could have paid him off. Somebody like him could cover up anything." Her eyes widened. "There are Delanceys on the police force."

"Whoa, slow down," Dawson said quickly, instinctively steering her away from Michael Delancey as the villain of the Golden Galaxy Casino tragedy. Trouble was, he wasn't sure she was wrong. He decided to press her for more information carefully.

"Why are you so convinced that Michael Delancey is the one responsible for the collapse?"

She looked at him steadily. "Because he built the casino. He was the contractor. Every design, every purchase order, every decision that was made went through him." She stopped and swallowed. "Whatever caused the Sky Walk to collapse and kill my father and five other people was approved by Michael Delancey."

Dawson nodded. Everything she said was true, and her conclusion was rational. He'd reached the same conclusion eight years ago when questions arose about the luxury condominiums his dad had been building in Chef Voleur. At that time Dawson had been working for his dad, but once accusations started flying about inferior materials, Dawson had bailed.

He'd already tired of physical labor anyway, so he'd moved to Biloxi and gone back to school for a Ph.D. in Criminal Justice. He, like his kid brothers, was interested in law enforcement, but unlike Ryker and Reilly, he did not want to work for someone else. So he'd gotten his private investigator license and opened his own business.

By that time, his dad was in prison, so John Dawson Delancey had registered his business under the name John D. Dawson and distanced himself from the infamous Delancey dynasty.

He realized Juliana was talking to him.

"Well?" she said impatiently. "You out there in ya-ya land. Do you want to see it or not?"

Dawson blinked. "Uh, yeah," he said, having no clue what she was referring to. "Sure."

She flipped through the folders and pulled out the flattest one. It couldn't have more than two sheets of paper in it. She opened it carefully and took out a plastic bag that contained a note.

Dawson's pulse hammered. "What's that?" He reached for it, but Juliana held on to it.

"You can look at it, but you can't take it out of the baggie. You can't touch the paper."

"No problem."

She handed him the plastic bag. He quickly scanned the note, written in carefully lettered block print.

BE CAREFUL, CAPRESE. THERE'S PROBLEMS WITH THE SKY WALK. DELANCEY SHOULD KNOW. LOOK AT VEGA. HE HOLDS GRUDGES.

"Where'd you get this?" he demanded sharply.

"It was in Daddy's wallet, under that little hidden flap in the bill compartment."

Dawson held it up to the light, studying it more closely. He turned the baggie over. "Look how creased it is. It must have been folded in your dad's wallet for weeks. See the wear on the creased edges?"

She nodded.

"Are you the one who bagged it?"

She nodded again. "I thought if there were any fingerprints on the paper, I didn't want to take a chance on smudging them."

"How much did you handle it?"

"I took it out of his wallet and unfolded it," she said. "Then when I realized what it was, I used kitchen tongs to slide it into the plastic bag."

"When did you find it?"

"The day before the funeral. I was looking for insurance papers, cards—you know, stuff the funeral home needed."

"And you don't have any idea when he got it?"

"No, he never mentioned it."

"When was the Sky Walk finished? The grand opening of the Golden Galaxy was in May, right?"

"June 1."

"What about the casino? Did your dad talk about it?"

She smiled sadly. "He was so excited about his new job. He'd managed other casinos, but the Golden Galaxy was the largest and the most elaborate. He was so proud of it, and it killed him." By the time she finished, her voice was tight and hoarse, laced with grief and thousands of unshed tears.

He laid his hand over her fist and gently urged her fingers to loosen. She was so rigid, so controlled. Her fingers finally relaxed.

He squeezed her hand reassuringly as he studied the note.

"Is this how you decided that Michael Delancey was responsible for what happened?"

"Yes, it's right there in black and white. *Delancey should know.*"

Dawson had his own opinion of what the three words meant. Was the writer saying that Delancey knew that something was wrong? Or was he saying that Delancey should be told about the note? There was no way to be sure.

"What about this reference to Vega?" He knew who Tito Vega was. He'd heard his dad talk about him for eight years. Michael blamed Vega for framing him and putting him in prison.

"The name sounded vaguely familiar to me, so I looked him up." Juliana flipped awkwardly through the folders in her lap and pulled one out. She opened it and glanced at the pages before she handed it to him. Probably checking to be sure there was nothing in there that she didn't want him to see.

The pages were printouts of webpages, articles and op-eds about Vittorio "Tito" Vega. Dawson skimmed them. She'd done a good job ferreting out information about the high-profile real-estate investor.

Dawson already knew a lot about him. Vega patronized the arts and enjoyed involving himself in local politics. He was an important contributor to both. But like many public figures, rumors abounded that he was involved in other, less laudable ventures. One of the regional newspapers occasionally printed op-ed pieces that suggested that Tito Vega was involved in loan-sharking and even bribery.

"What did Vega have to do with the Golden Galaxy?" he asked, although he already knew from his dad that Vega was somehow involved.

Juliana sat up, pride and excitement giving her cheeks a pretty pink blush. "It took me a long time to find that. He apparently worked very hard to keep his various concerns separate. It was really difficult to track them, but I did it!"

Dawson was impressed. He knew about Vega. He'd done his own investigation into Vega's activities after his dad went to prison. He'd tried to prove that his dad was telling the truth—that Vega had framed him. He'd failed, but he'd ended up with a file drawer full of information and a fairly long list of people who'd been hurt by the real-estate mogul.

"I finally put it all together." She dug out another folder and handed him a sheet of paper. "Take a look at this."

It was a handwritten flowchart. Vega's name was at the top and the Golden Galaxy Casino was at the bottom. Dawson followed the flow of companies down the chart. There were eight of them.

"Wow," he said. He recognized most of the companies, because he'd traced Vega's connection to the Golden Galaxy, too, but if he'd written out a chart like this, his would have had several holes in it. "This is impressive. I was working on something like this, but I didn't find any connection with Meadow Gold and I never heard of Bayside Industries."

Juliana beamed. "That was a hard one. It's actually a company based in Switzerland that makes knives. We export steel to them, then we buy the knives to sell here. It's the only one I'm not a hundred percent sure of. See here? Vittorio Vega, Inc. owns Biloxi Coast Realty and Islandview Condominiums in Bay St. Louis. The corporation manages a number of marinas along the Gulf Coast. It took me a while, but I found a marina in Pascagoula that was owned by Vega, Inc. but was sold a few years ago to Meadow Gold Corporation, which owns the Golden Galaxy."

Dawson was impressed. "You must have dug pretty deep to find that," he said.

She nodded. "Now, here's where it gets really interesting. I couldn't find any figures from the Pascagoula marina, but

Meadow Gold buys a lot of knives from Bayside Industries and sells them to that marina. And the last piece of the puzzle I could find was Avanti Investments. One of their holdings was the tract of land the Golden Galaxy is built on. They went bankrupt after Katrina, and Meadow Gold Corporation picked up the land for a song. Avanti had Bayside Industries in their stock portfolio. And that's how Vega is connected to the Golden Galaxy."

"And you can prove it?"

The triumphant blush left her cheeks and she looked down at her stack of folders. "I don't know. I copied all the public documents I could find, but some of it, like Avanti's stock portfolio, I only found one reference to that, and it was several years ago. So anywhere along the line, the connection could break down." She raised her gaze to his and her dark eyes glistened with tears. "I'm afraid it's not good enough. A lot of paperwork was lost in the storm surge."

She blinked and the dampness that had been clinging to her lower lashes spilled over onto her cheek. Dawson didn't realize he was going to catch it with his thumb until it was too late to stop himself.

Her eyes drifted closed when he brushed the tear away. It would be the easiest thing in the world to kiss her. He leaned forward, mesmerized by the thick dark lashes that threw spiky shadows onto her cheeks. His gaze moved to her mouth. Her lips were slightly parted. A blade of desire sliced through him and he reached for her.

His hand hit the stack of folders.

Her eyes flew open. She grabbed them up and hugged them to her chest.

Dawson pulled back, stunned.

Juliana bit her lip and carefully relaxed her left arm, wincing, but she still hung on to the folders with her right arm.

He stood and stared down at her. "You really think that's

what I was doing? Trying to distract you while I went for your little stack of research?" he asked harshly.

"I—" she looked beyond him, then down "—I didn't know. I mean, you say you're here to help me, but you haven't taken your eyes off the folders since you came in."

Dawson stepped away from the couch and grabbed his jacket. "Yeah, right," he said. He was pissed that she thought he was going to grab her paperwork and run. But he was also embarrassed. His ego was stinging. Not only had he ruined his chances of getting his hands on those folders, but he'd also given in to a stupid impulse and tried to kiss her.

"Look, Dawson, you're charming and—" she gestured toward him "—attractive, and I appreciate the information you gave me, but I'm trying to get justice for my dad. He didn't deserve to die. And the truth is, I don't know what you're trying to do."

Dawson nodded, holding on to his temper with an iron fist. "That's true. You don't." He shrugged into his jacket and stalked toward her front door and opened it. Then he turned back.

"You won't have to worry about me getting close enough to steal your little folders again. But make no mistake, Juliana Caprese, I'm riding your tail until you either find what you're looking for or give up." He opened the door and gave her his parting shot.

"There's no way in hell I'm going to sit by and let you get yourself killed."

# Chapter Five

Friday morning Juliana hurried down the steps from her apartment and into the waiting taxi. She wore jeans and low-heeled boots. There was no telling what kind of mess she'd be digging through.

Ten minutes later the driver said, "Here? This is where you wanna go?"

"Yes, right here. And I want you to wait for me," she said as she climbed out.

"No, no, no," he protested, shaking his head. "I'll lose too much money."

"Keep the meter running."

"That don't count for tips."

Juliana sighed. "I'll give you an extra twenty. I'll be out in less than a half hour."

The driver eyed her narrowly. "Fifty."

"Forty. Otherwise forget it."

"Okay, forty," he said, putting the vehicle in Park.

She looked at the expansive gaudy exterior of the Golden Galaxy Casino. It had been billed as the largest casino on the Mississippi Gulf Coast. Now it was the biggest piece of wreckage. The paper had said that demolition was scheduled to begin Monday. And this was Friday. That was why she was here.

Walking past the fountains and reflecting pools that surrounded the main entrance, Juliana saw the crosses and silk flowers families had placed. She hadn't brought one for her dad. She had no desire to memorialize this place that had killed him.

She ducked under the crime scene tape and dug into her pocket for her dad's key ring. There were two keys embossed with the Golden Galaxy logo. Her dad had brought her here before the casino opened to show her the Sky Walk, so she knew what the keys were for. She was worried about opening the electronic doors manually with her injured arm, but when she approached, they easily glided open. The electricity was on.

The interior wasn't as dark as she'd feared it might be. Sunlight shone through the glass doors and the glass-domed roof. The network of structural yet decorative metal beams that crisscrossed below the glass dome cast geometric shadows on the walls. Still, she was going to need more light to see her way through the wreckage and debris to her dad's office.

She glanced around. The electrical closet was to the right. She walked to the door and unlocked it. Inside the small space she couldn't see a thing. She fished her flashlight out of her oversized purse and shone it on the banks of gray metal boxes with black switches.

Squinting, she read the tiny labels. Most of them might as well have been written in Greek. But finally she found a row of labels that made sense. *Offices, Main, Bar, Restaurant 1, Restaurant 2, Sky Walk, Kitchen.* She switched on Offices and Main. Lights flared behind her.

With the lights on, she could see the rows of slot machines. They were all turned off, making them look like silent soldiers guarding the dead. Beyond them, the twisted remains of the Sky Walk glowed with what had to be half of the thirty million minilights that had made it the most spectacular architectural feature on the Gulf Coast.

The massive suspended walkway had stretched from the indoor parking garage on the west side of the casino, over the administrative offices and across the main casino floor. It had hung from the crisscrossed beams above it.

Patrons could walk directly from the garage across to the Milky Way Bar and the Pleiades Restaurant on the east end of the casino.

Tears clogged her throat and her chest tightened until she couldn't breathe. This was the first time she'd seen the wreckage.

But now she had to face it. She stepped up closer to the steel-and-chrome monster that had killed her dad, glass crunching beneath her boots. Reaching in her bag, she pulled out her camera and snapped pictures until tears made it impossible to see clearly enough.

For a few moments, she buried her face in her hands and sobbed quietly. She wasn't used to crying. She'd never experienced this kind of loss. She barely remembered her mother, who'd died when she was a toddler. But she'd had her daddy all her life.

Now she was alone. The emptiness in her chest ached as if her heart had been ripped right out of her.

She blotted her cheeks on her shirt sleeve and followed the line of the wreckage west, until the casino manager's office—her dad's office—came into sight. Her eyes stung again, but she swallowed determinedly and raised the camera.

The view screen brought the extent of the destruction into sharp, raw focus. Obviously, search-and-rescue crews had hauled away much of the shattered glass, wood and drywall in this area.

The tangle of rods and cables that had been the Sky Walk was peeled back like a pile of spaghetti pushed to one side of a plate. She knew that it had taken them several hours and some fancy equipment to get to her dad. He'd been working in his office early that morning.

He hadn't had a chance. According to the autopsy report, he'd died of blunt force trauma to his head when the wreckage collapsed the ceiling of his office. She supposed she should be thankful that he hadn't lingered, trapped there under the tangle of metal and debris.

Juliana blew out a long breath. *We've got to concentrate,* her little voice said. *If we keep crying we'll never get done.*

"I know," she whispered as she stiffened her back, lifted her chin and held the camera steady to snap a photo. Then she heard a sound.

Was that a leather shoe scraping on the marble floor? It had come from beyond her dad's office, from the west, the direction of the parking garage.

She held her breath, waiting for the second step, but it didn't come. Just about the time she'd decided her imagination was playing tricks on her, a solid echoing thump reverberated through the empty darkness, like the slamming of a door.

Her heart pounded in her throat and Dawson's voice echoed in her head.

*If you want to be a private eye, you can't let every little noise spook you. Use sound to evaluate your enemy.*

She forced herself to think rationally, like Dawson would. A shoe scraping, a door slamming. If that were even what the sounds were, they'd probably been made by some homeless guy. The door had sounded like one of the heavy metal ones that led to the parking garage.

She raised the camera and clicked off one, two, three shots of the Sky Walk. She aimed higher, to the rods that had held it suspended above the casino. Then she carefully maneuvered closer, wanting to include the wreckage of her dad's office in the next shot.

Another sound. This time from the other direction, to the east. She froze, listening, replaying the sound in her head. After a couple of seemingly endless seconds, she figured out what it was. The smooth glide of the glass door at the front entrance. Someone had come inside. Maybe a security guard or the police.

Her first thought was to hide. She could duck behind something and wait until he left. But cowering behind a slot machine or under a blackjack table like a child while the officer shone his light in her face didn't appeal to her. No, she'd face him like a man—a *woman*.

She couldn't see the main entrance from where she stood. She debated heading back that way—toward the sound. But she decided to wait, to see if she heard anything else. She listened, but the cavernous casino was quiet—eerily quiet.

What if it wasn't a guard or a cop? What if someone had followed her here? The same person who'd attacked her at the post office maybe?

She reached for her weapon. Slipping her left arm out of the sling, she used it to steady her right hand. And waited.

Suddenly she heard noises everywhere. From behind her, something scraped. She half turned. Was that another footstep or just a falling bit of debris? A creak echoed over her head. She winced and suppressed the instinctive urge to cower as she thought about the tons of steel above her that hadn't yet fallen.

Then she heard the unmistakable squeak of a sneaker. She whirled, aiming in the direction of the noise. Her heart thudded painfully in her tight chest, this time with fear.

The footsteps were soft, but the sneakers occasionally screeched as they scraped on the marble. Not a cop. Not anyone official.

*Private Security*

She didn't move, hardly dared to breathe as she counted, measuring the length of time between steps. The stride told her it was a man, a tall man—a confident, careful man.

The closer he came, the faster her heart pounded. The barrel of the gun wavered visibly in her shaking hands.

*If we want to be a private eye,* her little voice said, *we can't give in to fear. We need to use the adrenaline to clear our heads.*

"So now you're the expert?" she muttered, then took a deep breath and thumbed the safety off.

The click cracked through the air like a gunshot. The steps paused. Juliana's fingers tightened around the grip.

*Don't make me shoot,* she begged.

*Give me the courage to pull the trigger,* she prayed.

Then he, whoever he was, started walking again. A figure came into view, walking with a steady gait. Juliana's mouth went dry.

Backlit by the sunlight through the doors, he was a large, looming silhouette. He spotted her and stopped.

Fight-or-flight response sparked inside her like dozens of matches striking at once. Her finger tightened on the trigger. She gasped for breath. She widened her stance, balancing her weight on the balls of her feet, and aimed at the silhouette.

He started forward again.

"Hold it," she commanded, dismayed at the breathlessness in her voice. "Don't take another step or I'll shoot."

"Son of a bitch, rookie!" a disgustingly familiar voice snapped as long, leanly muscled arms rose. "I thought you had better sense."

Juliana ground her teeth together. It was Dawson. The blood surging through her now carried aggression, not fear. She spoke tersely. "What are *you* doing here?"

"What am I—" Dawson laughed harshly.

The sound shredded her raw nerves.

"Trying to keep your butt alive," he snapped, walking up to her and pushing the barrel of the gun away from his midsection. "Somebody ought to take that thing away from you—permanently."

She could see his face in the glow from the thousands of minilights. His brows were drawn down into a dangerous scowl, made more terrifying by the sharp shadows the tiny lights cast.

"I have a carry permit," she said, hating the lame whine in her voice.

"Now I feel better," he scoffed. "Put the damn thing away, and don't forget to put the safety on or you'll shoot your own butt off."

She meekly flipped on the safety and holstered her gun. "You followed me," she snapped accusingly, while at the same time feeling her face heat up. She should have noticed a car following the taxi.

In fact, she should have paid attention yesterday when he just happened to walk by in time to rescue her groceries. She hadn't even thought about checking out his vehicle. Damn it, she deserved to be called a rookie.

"Yeah, I did. If you want to be a private eye, you need to be able to spot a tail—and lose it."

"What did you do, stake out my apartment?"

"What if it hadn't been me? What if the guy who attacked you had walked in here instead? Did you really think you were going to shoot somebody?"

Embarrassed that he'd sneaked up on her, she snapped, "I was prepared to defend myself. I have that right."

"Not so much when you're the one trespassing," he pointed out. He grabbed her elbow. "Come on, I'm getting you out of here before somebody calls the police."

She jerked away. "No! I have to—" She stopped. "No. I'm fine."

"Still don't trust me, do you?" he said drily. "What did I tell you? If you want to be a private eye, you've got to learn to judge character."

"I'm a good judge of character," she snapped. "I just haven't seen anything to convince me that you're trustworthy."

His mouth tightened. "I gave you that information about the forensic engineer."

"Oh, please," she said. "Like I didn't already know it was going to take time to get that report back."

He gazed at her narrowly. "You didn't know about the preliminary findings."

He was right. Still, that didn't mean he could be trusted.

"What possessed you to come here anyway?" he asked. "What do you think you're going to find that the police haven't?"

"That's not why I'm here. The newspaper said they're going to start demolition Monday. I wanted to look around his office. There are some things of his that I haven't been able to find."

"It's still a crime scene. That's what the bright yellow tape outside means." He gave her a pensive look. "Speaking of which, did you turn on the electricity?"

"The electronic doors worked. I turned on the main casino and office lights. Nobody ever asked me for Daddy's keys."

Dawson nodded. "You should have locked the doors behind you."

"That's true. It would have kept you out." She turned and walked gingerly toward the office. Despite the cleanup, the floor was still littered with glass and chunks of drywall. The massive mahogany desk that sat in the middle of the room had been cracked in the middle, its polished surface scarred and covered with dust. Juliana brushed against a board and felt a nail scrape her calf. Thank goodness she'd worn jeans.

Dawson followed her, taking in the scene. "Look," he said. "That supply closet is still intact."

"Daddy was standing over there," she said, pointing directly opposite the closet. A few of the flat-screen security monitors still lay on the floor. They were smashed beyond repair. "The police told me he must have been looking at them…" Her voice gave out.

"Wow," Dawson whispered. He was craning his neck to follow the mess of steel and chrome that had formed the structure of the Sky Walk. "Look at how the metal is bent back on itself. They must have brought in a couple of Jaws of Life."

Juliana's heart lurched painfully and she squeezed her eyes shut for a moment. "Three," she said, her voice breaking. "The police told me."

"Sorry," Dawson muttered.

Her throat tightened and a small, strangled moan escaped. Dawson's hand squeezed her shoulder. Warmth seeped through her shirt to her skin and flowed all the way through her, warming places inside her that had been cold ever since her dad had died. Tears began to build again.

"Let's go," he said. "Let's get out of here. The police probably have all of your dad's things. I'll take you by the police station."

"No," she said. "I want to look for myself. They might have missed something." She turned to the broken desk, working to suppress the thought of how much more vulnerable a human body was than wood. She picked her way behind it. The large file drawers were on the floor, in pieces.

"Jules, don't do that."

She ignored him, retrieving her flashlight and bending to shine it inside and under the desk. "There's a folder and some papers back there. They must have been stuck behind the drawer."

She reached her right arm in, but the desk was too deep.

"Get out of the way," Dawson said. He took the flashlight from her, gauged the position of the papers, then reached in. He pulled out a torn hanging file folder with a few sheets of paper inside it.

Juliana wanted to sit down and go through them, but Dawson was right. They needed to get out of here. So she stuffed them into her purse.

Turning back to the desk, she tugged on the middle drawer, which was a quarter of the way open, but it wouldn't budge. "Can you get this drawer out for me?" she asked Dawson as he got to his feet.

"Watch out," he said. He pulled on the drawer. It barely gave, so he jerked it. With a loud shriek of wood against wood, it slid halfway and something flew out. Just as the noise faded, a metallic clunk echoed above their heads.

Dawson froze for a few fractions of a second.

"What—" Juliana started.

"Shh." He held up a hand, listening.

Juliana heard a quiet squeak, but that was all. Even though Dawson stood still listening for another few seconds, Juliana didn't hear anything else.

"Something's going on up there," he said grimly. "That's the second time I've heard that."

Juliana looked up. "What do you mean?"

He shrugged. "I don't know, but there's a reason the crime scene tape is still up and they're planning to demo the whole thing. It's dangerous in here."

Juliana was searching around on the floor for whatever had fallen out of the drawer. "Look," she said, picking up a familiar oblong box. "I knew this pen set was here some-where. I gave it to him." She looked at the initials she'd had engraved into the metal.

"What else is in there?" she muttered, feeling around in

the back of the drawer. She touched something that felt like smooth leather. When she pulled it out she saw that it was a pocket-size photo album she'd given him when she was in high school. She'd had it engraved with his initials. She touched the gold letters and felt tears start in her eyes. Blinking them away, she opened it. The first picture was her school portrait from her sophomore year in high school. She remembered deciding to stop wearing her hair that way as soon as she saw the proofs.

The next one was a picture of her at around age six, judging by her gap-toothed grin. She tried to swallow the anguished moan that rose to her lips, but it slipped out.

Dawson took the album from her and stuffed it into her bag. "You can look at that later," he muttered.

She blinked and looked back at the drawer. She reached inside it and felt all the way to the back. Her fingers touched another smooth rectangle. It was her dad's day planner. He'd always carried one. When she was little, he'd let her doodle on the blank pages in the back. This one had sticky notes tucked inside the back cover, all covered with her dad's handwriting.

"Oh," she whispered wistfully. He'd always used sticky notes to jot down information about his employees. She'd asked him once why he didn't just put the information in his day planner.

*These are incidents in an employee's day,* he'd told her. *What if he is having a bad day, and by tomorrow he's performing like a pro? Or on the other hand, what if a great employee suddenly changes—becomes surly or lackadaisical?*

Dawson looked up. "What's all that?" he asked.

"Daddy's day planner for this year."

Dawson took it and stuffed it into her bag. "That'll wait until later, too. Ready to go?"

"No," she said as she felt around one last time. Just as she'd decided the drawer was empty, she touched something cold and hard. She pulled it out.

"Oh," she whispered. "It's his wedding ring. I wondered where it was." She slipped the ring onto her thumb and then her middle finger but it was too large. The wedding ring was the last straw. The tears were suddenly falling faster than she could dash them away, her throat ached with grief and she felt sobs gathering in her chest.

She clenched her fist around the ring and lifted her chin. She knew what Dawson was thinking. *P.I.s don't cry.* Well, that was tough. She wasn't a P.I. yet. She was just what he'd called her—a rookie.

# Chapter Six

Juliana dashed tears away and waited for Dawson's sarcastic jab. But instead, he laid his hand on her shoulder again, spreading his comforting warmth.

She wanted to act professional, like a private investigator would, but this was where her dad had died. She ducked her head as Dawson took her in his arms.

He didn't say anything. He just held her comfortingly. He rubbed her back, moving his gentle hand up and down, up and down.

As her sobs began to fade, Dawson's hand moved downward, toward the small of her back and the pressure changed. Not much. Hardly enough to notice, but definitely different.

His touch was no longer comforting, she realized. In fact, it was becoming noticeably sensual. His other hand, which had cradled the back of her head, now slid down to the nape of her neck and his thumb lightly caressed the curve of her jaw.

She pulled back slightly and looked up at him. His gaze was soft. A tiny smile, not sarcastic at all, curved his lips.

"How're you doing?" he whispered. His fingers slid across her skin until they rested against the side of her neck and his thumb grazed her lower lip. That unconsciously erotic gesture stoked an awareness deep within her. She felt her body softening, changing. The awareness became a disturbingly sweet heat. She knew what he was about to do and she felt no compulsion to stop him. She was hurting and his touch was dissolving the pain.

She lifted her head and her gaze drifted downward to his mouth. He had a nice mouth, wide and straight. It could set firmly or curve sarcastically, but right now it was soft, like his eyes.

He bent his head. His thumb moved to her chin and pressed gently, urging her head to tilt a fraction higher. Then his lips brushed hers. Matches struck and flared inside her again. But this rush was neither flight or fight. It was desire.

He pulled her closer, molded her body to his as his mouth met hers. Her mouth softened and she parted her lips. She felt the whisper of his breath as he gasped. Then he deepened the kiss, and swept her away from the harsh reality of her dad's death and her single-minded search for an explanation. She was helpless against the confusing mix of feelings gushing through her.

Dawson had done his best not to give in to the hunger that gripped him every time he touched Juliana—hell, every time he laid eyes on her. But he was a sucker for tears, like his dad. That thought nearly killed the desire, but just then her mouth moved sensuously and her tongue touched his and his rational thoughts scattered like shards of an exploding lightbulb.

His libido urged him to lay her down right here in the dust and debris, but his brain warned him of the sheer stupidity of letting his desire do the thinking.

Placing a hand on either side of her head, he drew back and gazed down at her. He ran his thumb lightly along the fading bruise on her cheek and she blinked and stared up at him. Her eyes were so dark. They absorbed the light like black velvet. He kissed the corners of her eyelids where tears still clung and tasted salt.

"We should—" he started, but a loud metallic screech

drowned out his words. Without stopping to think, he grabbed Juliana and dove through the open closet door. He twisted in midair, trying to take the brunt of the impact. His shoulder slammed against the floor.

A deafening crash shook the walls and sent splinters, debris and dust flying. Dawson hunched his shoulders and rolled, putting his back to the destruction. He wrapped his arms around her head and ducked his.

He waited until the last echoing thump died down and the walls stopped quivering before lifting his head and opening his eyes. He looked down at her. He didn't dare move until he was sure she was okay.

She was stiff as a board, her face buried in his shirt. Despite her rigidity, he could feel the fine trembling of her limbs and the hitch in her breathing.

"Jules?" he whispered anxiously.

Her body jerked and she slowly lifted her head. Her eyelids twitched, then fluttered. Relief gushed through him.

"Dawson?" she whispered as she opened her eyes, then blinked. "What happened?"

"Are you okay?" he asked. "Can you move?"

She closed her eyes and gingerly tested her arms and legs. "Ow," she said. "My shoulder hurts, but I think that's all."

He sat up carefully.

"What happened?" she asked, then, "Oh, my God!"

Dawson looked over his shoulder and saw the source of the crash. A two-foot-wide metal I beam lay across what was left of the mahogany desk. Where before it had been broken in two, now it was smashed flat.

"We were—" Juliana gasped.

"Standing right there," he said grimly. He craned his neck and looked up. He knew from the architect drawings his dad had given him that the main floor of the casino with its three-story-high glass-domed roof was flanked on three sides by restaurants, guest rooms, offices and conference rooms and on the fourth side by the enclosed parking garage. The Sky Walk had arced over the main floor, suspended from the grid of beams just like the one in front of them.

He pushed himself to his feet and carefully approached the I beam. It lay parallel to the closet. He shuddered involuntarily as he measured its length with his eyes. If it had swung ninety degrees before crashing, he and Juliana would be dead.

What the hell had made it fall? Pulling out his key ring, he shone his laser light along the metal surface. He leaned in and there it was. What he saw took his breath away.

"Son of a—" He tensed. Instinctively, he held his breath and listened, rocking to the balls of his feet.

His first impulse was to race out and chase down the man who'd sent the beam crashing down on them, but it had been at least twenty seconds, probably thirty, since the beam had fallen. Whoever did it had a half minute's head start. Besides, he couldn't leave Juliana here alone.

He pulled his phone from his pocket to call 9-1-1, but there was no signal.

Behind him, Juliana groaned as she got to her feet. She stepped up close to him and placed her hand on his arm. "Oh, my God, we could have been killed," she whispered.

He didn't answer.

"Dawson, look at those bolts." She pointed. "Shine the light there."

He knew what she'd seen—the same thing he had.

"They've been cut," she gasped.

"Yeah," he said. "Come on, we need to get out of here." He put his hand on the small of her back.

She didn't budge. "I want to get a picture of that."

"Jules, the guy who did this is probably long gone, but I'm not willing to bet our lives on it. We need to be outside." He showed her his phone. "I tried to call the police, but I can't get a signal in here."

"Okay. Just a minute." Juliana was digging in her bag for her camera.

Dawson didn't object. He wanted photos of the beam as badly as she did. Not only to study, but also to show his dad. He figured the cuts had been made by bolt cutters, but he wanted his dad's opinion. Plus, he liked the idea of having proof, if they had been cut.

After she'd snapped several shots, Dawson touched her arm. "Let's go. Now!"

They picked their way past the beam and out onto the main floor of the casino, then headed for the main entrance. Dawson heard the sound of the doors gliding open. Then suddenly, there were two uniformed officers with guns and bright flashlights raised.

"Don't move," the lead officer shouted. "Get your hands up. Higher. Above your heads."

"She can't—" Dawson started, but the officer cut him off.

"Shut up and get those hands up," he shouted. "You, ma'am, take your arm out of that sling."

Juliana glanced toward Dawson, but he didn't want to do anything to antagonize the officers. He nodded.

She eased her arm out of the sling and raised it until her hand was level with her shoulder. He heard her muffled moan.

The officer was apparently satisfied. "Now walk over here. Slowly. And keep those hands up."

A second officer held his gun on Juliana while the first one covered Dawson.

"Who else is in here?" he demanded.

"No one." Dawson knew he wouldn't get anywhere trying to explain what they were doing here until the officers had disarmed them and gotten them out of the building.

The lead officer spoke into his shoulder mic. "I have two intruders at the Golden Galaxy Casino. Meeker and I will walk them out. Have the car ready to take them in for questioning. Send Stewart and Simon to clear the building."

Meeker gestured with his gun for them to pass him and take the lead. "Let's go," he said. "Keep those hands up. Either one of you makes a sudden move and I will shoot you."

JULIANA SAT IN the interrogation room of the Waveland, Mississippi, Police Department, trying not to look at the one-way mirror that covered the upper half of one wall. She'd been fidgeting for over an hour, imagining detectives and assistant district attorneys standing on the other side of the glass, watching her.

Instead, she concentrated on identifying the dingy color on the walls. Did they paint the walls such a vomit-green on purpose? Because between the wall color and the creepy mirror, she was almost ready to confess to anything just to get out of there.

The door opened and a young officer brought in a paper bag from a fast-food restaurant. "Hope you're not a vegetarian," he said with a smile. Juliana managed to get down about half a hamburger and was drinking the watery cola when the door opened again.

A medium-height, pleasant-looking man came in. He looked tired as he sat down and took a small pad out of his inside coat pocket. He had a pen in his hand and he clicked it as he flipped pages.

"I'm Detective Brian Hardy," he said. "You're—"

As soon as she heard his voice, she recognized him. "Juliana Caprese, but you already know that."

He nodded. "I spoke with you on June 20, the day your dad was killed."

She nodded. "You were very nice."

The look he gave her told her he wasn't in the mood to be nice today. He clasped his hands on the table. "Ms. Caprese, what were you doing at the Golden Galaxy?"

Just like the day of her dad's death, he got straight to the point. She felt her face heat up. "I'd rather not say," she said.

Hardy's eyebrows shot up. "Well, I'm afraid you don't have that option. We've looked at the contents of your purse—"

She frowned in surprise. "You can do that?"

Hardy's mouth turned up. "We had probable cause, considering that you were trespassing at an active crime scene. And considering that we found items taken from there—" Hardy flipped more pages. "Specifically an album, a day planner and a hanging file folder."

"How do you—" She clamped her mouth shut, but Hardy grinned.

"How do I know those were the items you took? Okay, well, they appeared to belong to your father." He held up his index finger. "They were in your purse." He held up a second finger. "And they were smeared with drywall dust. Now, I'm going to ask you one more time. What were you doing there?"

Juliana sighed. "I heard that demolition was going to begin Monday. I wanted to see if the police—if you had left any of my father's things there." She shrugged and spread her hands. "I wanted them. I'm sure you saw that the album has pictures in it, and the day planner—it's his writing, his notes and thoughts and the things that made up his day."

Hardy was watching her closely. "So CSI missed those items and you found them."

"I'm his daughter," she said, tears welling in her eyes. "Why are you wasting time with me? Why aren't you finding out who was responsible for his death?"

"We are. In fact, I need to ask you about what happened while you were in the casino."

"You've got the statement I wrote," Juliana said. "Everything that happened is in there." She assessed him. "Did you look at that beam? The bolts were cut. It was obvious. I took photos of the bolts. For evidence. My camera's in my purse."

Hardy's mouth turned up again. "As it happens, our CSI team is taking photos, too. We'll be investigating what happened to cause that beam to fall. Were you aware that you were being followed?"

"Followed?" She figured he wasn't talking about Dawson. "You mean the person who dropped the beam on us? No. Dawson would have known. He'd have told me." Speaking of Dawson, where was he? She glanced toward the door, then back at Detective Hardy. Just as she was about to ask, Hardy spoke.

"What happened to your arm? And your face?" he asked.

She touched her cheek. "I fell," she said shortly.

"You fell," he repeated, raising his brows. "That must have been some fall. What happened?"

Juliana didn't want to tell the detective about her attack. She was afraid he'd order her to stop her investigation, and she wasn't about to do that. "It was an accident," she said, hoping she sounded convincing. "I tripped and fell down the stairs."

"Hmm," Hardy said.

He didn't believe her. She lifted her chin. "I hit my shoulder."

"Juliana, why would someone want to harm you?"

She swallowed and shook her head. "Maybe someone thinks I know who was responsible for the Sky Walk collapsing."

"Do you?"

She hesitated an instant too long and saw Hardy's eyes narrow. "No. How would I know?"

"Now that's a very good question. I'm still interested in how you found those items after CSI missed them."

"It wasn't that hard, Detective. They were in the back of the desk drawer. I found them because I knew they had to be there."

"And the keys to the casino doors and the electrical closet? Where did you just know they had to be?"

Juliana dropped her gaze to her hands. "The doors opened automatically."

"Are you aware that it is a crime to withhold evidence?"

She nodded.

"Well, since these items aren't related to the investigation, we're going to release them to you. But tell me, is there anything else of your father's I should know about?" he asked.

She sent the detective a narrow gaze. "No." She took a deep breath. "Am I going to be charged with something?"

Hardy rose, and his chair screeched on the floor. "Not this time. But Juliana, don't go back there. If you do and you make it out alive, I *will* put you in jail."

## *Chapter Seven*

Dawson shook Detective Hardy's hand. "Thanks, Brian," he said. "I appreciate your helping me out with this."

Hardy gave him a sour look. "I don't like it."

Dawson understood. Detective Brian Hardy had been in Vice when Dawson's dad was indicted eight years ago. It was Hardy's dogged determination that had finally convinced Michael to accept a plea bargain for three years in prison rather than go to trial and risk a much longer sentence.

"Well, you're the one who told me I could call on you any time if I needed a favor."

"I was thinking more along the lines of helping you with a criminal case, not hiding your identity from a beautiful woman whose father just died. I don't like lying to her."

"It's not lying exactly."

"Lying by omission is still lying," Hardy said. "I had to sit there in front of her and deliberately not talk about you. Several times I was sure she was going to ask me why I hadn't mentioned you."

"It's your own fault. If y'all won't put her in protective custody, I'm the only one who can protect her."

"So protect her. I can't do anything until I get confirmation from the Forensics team that the I beam's bolts were cut."

"That beam didn't fall on its own. And before you say

anything, I know she was followed." Dawson grimaced. "I didn't spot the tail."

Hardy assessed him. "Yeah, when I asked her if she knew she'd been followed, she said no. Said you'd have spotted the tail and told her. Are you sure this case isn't getting a little personal for you?"

"Sure it's personal. My dad's under investigation."

"Right. That's not exactly what I'm talking about."

"She's in danger. You saw how banged up she is. She was attacked and a letter was stolen from her."

"She said she tripped on the stairs."

Dawson couldn't suppress a smile. "Well, technically that's true, but as an eyewitness to her fall, I can testify that she had the bruises, the sling and a banged-up knee prior to falling down two steps."

Hardy narrowed his gaze at Dawson. "Tell me about the letter."

Dawson clenched his jaw. Maybe he shouldn't have mentioned it. "She put an ad in the paper."

"That ad was hers? The ten-thousand-dollar reward?"

"I'm surprised you hadn't already figured that out."

"Nope. I was going to put a guy on it, but I had to pull him to work another homicide." He paused for a beat. "What's her angle?"

Dawson rubbed his hand across the back of his neck. He wasn't sure how much he wanted to tell Brian. He sure didn't want him sniffing around his dad's heels again. "I'm in a bind here. She's beginning to trust me. If she finds out I'm a Delancey, she won't let me near her." Dawson shook his head. "I can't let that happen."

"And why is that?"

Dawson almost growled in frustration. Hardy knew the answer to that. He was just giving him a hard time.

"She's out to prove that someone is responsible for the Sky Walk falling. She wants justice for her father's death."

"Let me guess. She thinks it was your dad."

Dawson nodded. "That's right. She's convinced that he skimped on the Sky Walk to make a bigger profit."

"Well, she can join the club. A lot of people think that."

"Including you?"

"I believe in innocent until proven guilty," Hardy hedged, eyeing him closely. "What do you think?"

"I don't know." Dawson heard the defeat and doubt in his voice. "I don't think so."

"You were convinced your dad was guilty eight years ago."

"Yeah, I was a lot younger and I was tired of working for him." Dawson paused for a beat. Then he shrugged. "I have the resources now to do my own investigation. I need to know the truth about my dad. And Juliana has information that I need."

"And that's the only reason you're so hell-bent on sticking to her?" Hardy didn't sound convinced.

Dawson shook his head. "Look at her. She's going to get herself killed. I'll tell you this," he said, lifting a finger toward Hardy. "My dad didn't have her assaulted and he didn't drop that beam."

Hardy scowled. "I told you, even if there is proof that the beam's bolts were cut, I don't have the resources to keep her under guard."

"Which is why I need you to keep my real name out of this. Luckily, I didn't know any of the officers at the scene."

Hardy nodded reluctantly. "Well, they're searching the casino and gathering evidence. I'll let you know if they turn up anything."

"Thanks, Brian." Dawson looked past him toward the interrogation rooms. "When are you going to be finished with her?"

"She should be signing her transcribed statement now. She'll be out any second."

"Mind if I make a phone call?"

"Nope."

Dawson pressed a speed-dial button on his phone and walked a few steps away from Detective Hardy. "Mack, anything on what I gave you to work on last night?" He was being vague deliberately. He didn't want anybody at the police station to pay attention to what he said.

"So I take it you can't talk freely," Mack said. "I got through to the secretary to one of the vice presidents. She's single."

"That's the information you have for me. She's single?" Dawson smiled. Typical Mack.

"There's a method here. I'm thinking I'd have better luck if I went there in person. You know I work best face-to-face."

Dawson chuckled. He definitely knew that. Mack could charm the hairpins out of a spinster's French twist without touching the pins or the spinster. "It's Friday."

"No problem. I've already hinted that I'd like to buy her dinner if she's not busy. And maybe go skiing Sunday."

"I wasn't going to spend that much—" Dawson started when he saw Juliana out of the corner of his eye. She looked tired and sad and bewildered. An odd feeling settled in the middle of his chest. He rubbed it absently.

"What the hell," he continued. "Go ahead, but you'd better pack plenty of charm because I want proof of a connection. Got it?"

"Sure, boss."

Dawson sighed. He had three investigators on his payroll. Two were exceptional. But they ate MacEllis Griffin's dust.

If anyone could connect Tito Vega with Bayside Industries, it was Mack. The question that Dawson couldn't answer was, would that connection help either Juliana or him accomplish their goals? He sure hoped so.

While he talked with Mack, a policewoman had given Juliana a clipboard to sign, then handed over her purse.

She looked around. Her gaze landed on him.

He let his mouth curve slightly in a smile. She didn't smile back. She put the bag over her shoulder and strode toward him. The dust on her jeans and the smudges on her face enhanced, rather than detracted from, the dignified tilt of her head.

She walked straight up to Hardy. "Am I free to go now?" she asked icily.

"For now," Hardy said. "But don't leave town, and remember what I said. I *will* toss you in jail."

She turned to Dawson. "Are you ready?"

"Yes, ma'am," he replied, lifting his hand in a mock salute.

BY THE TIME JULIANA climbed into Dawson's car and glanced at the dashboard clock, it was almost seven o'clock. "I'm so tired. I'm ready to get home and take a shower and go to bed."

Dawson didn't say anything. He just drove.

"Why didn't you tell me my taxi was followed to the casino?" she asked after a couple of minutes of silence.

He glanced at her sidelong. "Because I didn't know."

"I thought you said a private investigator—"

"I missed him, okay? And yes, that kind of mistake can get the client killed." He lifted his chin. "I'm sorry."

"I wasn't after an apology—"

"You deserve one for that. I could have stopped him from nearly killing you."

"Us," she amended, then fell silent. After a couple of minutes, she saw that he wasn't headed toward her apartment.

"Where are we going?" she asked. "I don't feel like—"

"Post office," he told her. "I want to check that box. You've got the key, don't you?"

"Yes." She looked at him. He was driving with one hand on the wheel. He looked relaxed, in total contrast to how she felt. She was dirty, tired, on edge and irritable.

"Aren't you tired?" she asked grumpily.

"I guess," he said. "I know I'm hungry."

"I was hungry several hours ago," she replied. "Now I just feel queasy and exhausted. Where did they keep you?"

He glanced at her sidelong. "Keep me?"

"Were you in an interrogation room, too? That had to be the most depressing room I've ever been in." She shuddered. "I almost confessed just to get out of there."

"Confessed?" Dawson said with a chuckle. "To what?"

"Anything. Everything."

Dawson pulled up to the curb of the post office where she'd rented the box. As he killed the engine, she reached into her bag and pulled out her keys. "I'll be right back," she said, reaching for the door, but Dawson caught her hand and took the keys from her.

"You're not going in there. I'll check the box. Number 7874, right?"

"You think that guy's watching?"

"I just don't want to take any chances." Dawson got out of the car and locked the doors, then disappeared into the building. Within a few seconds he was back out.

"Nothing?" she asked.

"Oh, yeah, there was something," he said, handing her keys back to her. He cranked the car and pulled away.

"What? Another letter?"

"Yep," he said noncommittally.

"Well? Give it to me," Juliana said. "I want to read it. Did you open it?"

He shook his head. "No. It's a federal offense to open someone else's mail."

She laughed nervously. "Let me have it." She reached over and patted his right coat pocket. "Where is it?"

"Stop that," he said, frowning. "I'm trying to drive."

"Then give me the letter."

"We'll look at it together," he said, sending her a quelling glance, "when we get home."

Dawson walked her to her door, still uncharacteristically silent. Once they were inside, she turned to him.

"Let me have my letter."

He shook his head.

"Dawson, isn't withholding mail a federal offense, too?"

"Get some things together. You're going to stay at my apartment for a few days."

"No, I'm not," she said. That would be a bad idea for several reasons.

"Look, Jules," he said, catching her arm. "I asked the detective to put you into protective custody until they could figure out who dropped that beam on our heads, but he said he doesn't have the manpower to guard you. So until they catch the guy, you're staying with me."

"I don't want to stay with you," she protested. "Does this have something to do with that letter?"

"No. Now come on." He stalked past her to the coffee table and picked up the file folders stacked there. "Get some clothes or don't, but you are coming with me."

"Put those down." She glared at him, but he was walking to the door. "Those are mine. You can't—"

"I'll just put them in the car."

"No, wait." She could tell by the look on his face that he was not bluffing. She couldn't let him walk out with her research. Every bit of evidence she had that the Sky Walk was defective was in those folders. Plus, he was holding hostage a response to her ad.

Her little voice protested. *We can't trust him, remember? And we are not capable of rational thought when he gets too close. Are we sure we want to sleep under the same roof?*

*We don't know,* she answered silently. Then out loud to Dawson, "Please just wait right there. I'll get some clothes."

Within ten minutes, when she came out of her bedroom with a weekender bag, Dawson was still standing at the door with the folders cradled in one arm, looking bored.

"Okay," she said. "I'm ready, but this is only for a day or two, right?"

"We'll see."

She glared at him. "You are such a bully. You think you're always right, so you don't even have to explain yourself. I'm going with you, but only because there's no way I'm letting you steal my research."

"I understand," he said solemnly, but she saw a twinkle in his eye.

She stormed past him, pulling the wheeled bag behind her, and threw the door open. "Bully," she said as she jerked the bag over the threshold.

DAWSON DROVE TO HIS CONDO in silence. Juliana sat in the passenger seat, her arms filled with her precious folders. She wasn't talking, which was fine with him. He had some thinking to do.

The letter he'd pulled from her post office box was burning a hole in the breast pocket of his jacket. The precise, architectural lettering on the envelope was branded on his inner vision. Except for the bars on the *A,* the *H* and the *T,* the words could have been written by any architect in the country. But those crossbars were unique. They slanted upward with a slight curve at the top edge. The envelope in his pocket had been addressed by Michael Delancey, his dad.

*What the hell are you doing, Dad?* His fist clenched on the steering wheel. He clamped his jaw, quelling the urge to slap the wheel with the heel of his palm.

He turned into the condos and drove around to his unit, opened the garage door, pulled inside and killed the engine.

"Here we are," he said, looking at her armful of folders. "I guess I'll get your bag."

"Fine," she snapped. She shifted the folders into her left arm and reached for the door handle, wincing.

"Hang on," he said on a sigh. He climbed out of the driver's side and went around and opened the door for her. "Can you climb the stairs with that armload?" he asked wryly.

"Yes."

"Good." He pulled her weekender bag out of the backseat and carried it up the stairs that led to his condo. "Come on, let's get cleaned up."

In the kitchen, he shrugged out of his jacket, then pointed toward the hall. "The bathroom is the first door on the right. The guest bedroom is the second. The second door on the left is my room."

She looked at him suspiciously, then headed down the hall, still carrying the folders. He followed with her bag.

"Here you go," he said. "Sorry I don't have a lock for the door."

Glaring at him, she set the folders down on the bed and set her bag down beside them. "Thank you," she said dismissively.

He smiled and backed out of the room. In his bedroom, he shed his own dirty clothes and tossed them onto the floor of the closet.

He heard the bathroom door close and not much later, the shower come on. The vision of Juliana in his shower, naked, using his soap and shampoo, rose before his eyes and he almost gasped as his body reacted immediately and powerfully.

For a few seconds, he closed his eyes and enjoyed that vision. Then he thought about the letter and the erotic daydream died instantly.

He glanced around for a second before he remembered he'd hung his jacket on a chair in the kitchen, like he usually did. The letter was in the pocket.

He opened the door to the hall and listened. The shower was still running. So he dashed up the hall in nothing but boxer shorts and grabbed the jacket. As he did he heard the water go off.

*Damn it.* He jogged toward his bedroom, figuring she still had to dry off and do stuff to her hair and whatever else women did. But as he passed the bathroom door, it opened and he was cloaked in a cloud of warm steam.

Juliana almost ran into him. "Oh," she said.

He put out a hand to steady her, but she stopped in time.

"What? You're na—" She gulped.

"Yeah," he said, giving her an apologetic shrug. "Sorry." He tried—he really tried—not to notice that she'd belted his terry cloth so tightly that it gaped at the neck. He tried not to look at the stunning view of her damp chest or the tops of her shapely breasts. He dragged his gaze away and looked down.

His turn to gulp. He saw her pink-tipped toes. *Toes.* Pretty sexy toes. A surge of desire nearly knocked him to his knees.

She pulled the collar of the robe together and took a step backward. When he met her gaze, her face and neck turned pink.

"I'll—just—you know, take my shower now," he said, swallowing hard. In about one second he was going to embarrass himself. He held the jacket in front of him as he stepped around her.

"Do you want your robe?"

*Yes,* his body screamed. *No!* his rational brain interrupted. Without turning around, he shook his head and jerked his thumb toward his room. "I'll get— I'll—manage."

"Please do. Meanwhile, I'm going to drink a gallon of water," she said and turned toward the kitchen.

Relieved that she had her back to him, he ducked into his room. For an instant, he looked at his jacket. Did he dare open the letter? No, not if he wanted her to trust him.

Grabbing a T-shirt and a pair of jeans and fresh underwear, he ducked across the hall into the bathroom and closed the door. It was still steamy from her shower. He climbed into the stall and stood there, letting the wet heat soak into his skin for a minute as his brain taunted him with visions of her.

These visions involved wet, slick, shiny skin and his robe, but instead of being pulled tight around her, it was hanging from her shoulders. Her ripe-peach skin was radiant in contrast to the white cloth.

He took a long shuddering breath, then grimaced and turned on the cold water.

## Chapter Eight

When Juliana set her water glass down, it rattled and almost turned over. She was *not* shivering with reaction from seeing Dawson ninety-percent naked. Because those boxers couldn't have covered more than ten percent of his body—his gorgeous naked body.

She'd been shocked when she'd opened the bathroom door and nearly run into him, but not too shocked that her body didn't react. It had taken all her willpower to keep from splaying her fingers across his broad chest.

Thank goodness she'd instinctively stepped backward, away from his hand, because if he'd touched her right then, she might have dropped the robe and her inhibitions onto the hall floor.

The vision of the two of them intertwined, their bodies glistening with steam, rose up before her eyes and a thrill rippled through her, centering itself in her core.

Dawson was strong and smart and protective—everything a girl could ever want, all rolled up into one gorgeous sexy package. And he was a private eye, which for her just made him sexier.

But once in a while, when he wasn't aware of her watching him, she caught a look in his eyes that she couldn't quite define. It was a hooded, shadowy look, like guilt or embarrassment—or deceit.

It worried her because like it or not, she needed him. Not only did he have resources she didn't have, but he was also definitely nice to have around to whisk her out of the way of deadly falling objects.

She just had to make sure she didn't get sidetracked by sex, that was all. At that thought, the thrill within her morphed into yearning.

"Here you are," Dawson said, startling her.

She almost didn't have the courage to turn around. The warm clean scent of hot water and soap wafted toward her. She took a deep breath to fortify herself, but all it fortified was the yearning inside her.

*Please be dressed.* She turned around. Relief cascaded through her. He had on worn jeans and a black New Orleans Saints T-shirt with a gold fleur-de-lis on the front. His hair was damp and brushed back from his freshly shaved face and—she gulped as she looked down.

He was barefooted.

If there was anything Juliana liked more than long sinewy bodies and beautiful hands, it was bony, sexy bare male feet peeking out from under frayed blue jeans.

"Jules?"

She blinked and looked up at him. He was smiling.

"Don't call me that," she protested weakly.

"Did you want to look at that letter?"

"Yes!" How had she forgotten about the letter? Sadly, she knew how. Because she'd been fantasizing about Dawson naked.

"Yes, definitely. Where is it?"

"It's in my jacket pocket. I'll get it." He headed back down the hall toward his room.

Juliana couldn't take her eyes off him. His skin looked golden under the hall lights. The contours of his back were elegantly masculine, following the curve of his spine down to the low-slung waistband of his jeans.

And those jeans, they cupped his butt perfectly—not too tight and not too loose. *Perfect.* When he appeared in his bedroom doorway and headed back up the hall, Juliana realized she had hardly blinked.

She cleared her throat and turned away, filling her water glass. She turned it up a little too quickly and spilled some down the front of the robe between her breasts. She shivered.

"Okay, here we are." He sat down at the kitchen table.

Juliana swiped away the droplets of water as she sat down next to him and took the letter.

She looked down at it, then up at Dawson. His gaze was on it and that odd, guilty look was shadowing his eyes again.

She slid her finger along the flap and then used two fingers to pull out the single sheet of paper. "It's copy paper. Looks like a regular sheet torn in half, then folded." She unfolded it and read the handwritten note.

YOU'RE ON THE RIGHT TRACK. VEGA'S CAPABLE OF ANYTHING. YOU'LL NEED PROOF, THOUGH. TALK TO KNOBLOCK.

"That's all it says?" Dawson asked, reaching for the paper.

"That's it." Juliana let him take it.

He stared at it for about twenty seconds, much longer than he needed to. He rubbed the paper between his fingers, held it up to the light, turned it over and looked at the back. "Do you know who Knoblock is?" he asked.

She shook her head. "I'm not sure. The name doesn't sound familiar. I was going to ask you. What about the handwriting?" she asked. "That's a peculiar printing style."

He nodded and turned the sheet back over. "Architectural printing."

"Architectural—you mean literally used by architects? Maybe it's the architect who designed the casino."

Dawson didn't answer.

"Or Michael Delancey? Wasn't he an architect before he went to prison?"

Dawson shook his head without looking up. "Good question," he said gruffly. Then he looked at his watch and stood. "I've got an appointment. If you're hungry, there's a frozen pizza in there." He gestured toward the refrigerator.

"You've got an appointment now?" Juliana asked. "But it's after eight o'clock."

"I have to go by my client's schedule." He adjusted his wristwatch.

"Is it about the Sky Walk?" she asked, frowning at him. Why did he suddenly look nervous?

"In a way. So, do you want to fix the pizza or should I bring you something back?"

She shook her head. "I'm not hungry. I ate that hamburger at the police station." She stood. "I want to go with you. I'll get dressed."

Dawson's head jerked as if she'd slapped him. "No!" he snapped, then, "No. How many times do I have to tell you I guarantee my clients' anonymity. If you want to be a private eye—"

"Yeah, yeah," she said, holding up her hands. "I get it. 'If I want to be a private eye, I need to protect my client's identity,'" she said mockingly.

Dawson shot her a look that was tinged with amusement. "That's right," he said.

"Fine. I'm exhausted anyway. I'll probably go to bed pretty soon."

He nodded. "I should be back in a couple of hours. I'll lock the door behind me. Take your cell phone with you. Don't answer the landline and don't open the door for anybody."

Apprehension sent her pulse racing. "Are you expecting someone to come to the door?" she asked.

"No, but—"

"I'll take my gun with me."

Dawson looked pained. "I'm still considering taking that thing away from you. Please try not to shoot yourself or any of my neighbors."

It wasn't until after he was gone that Juliana realized he'd taken the letter with him.

"WHAT THE HELL IS THIS?" Dawson tossed the letter toward his dad's lap. Michael Delancey caught it in midair, then set it on the table beside his chair.

He managed to look scared, desperate, guilty, embarrassed and indignant, all at the same time. "Son—"

"Don't give me excuses," Dawson snapped. "Give me answers for once. Do you have any idea what could have happened if the police had intercepted this letter?"

"The police? How would they get it? And how would they know it came from me?"

Dawson hissed. "Your prints are on file—and your DNA. Did you handle the paper with your bare hands? Did you lick the envelope to seal it?"

His dad squirmed and looked sheepish.

"What the hell did you think this would accomplish?"

Michael Delancey looked up at Dawson. "I *thought* I was giving Caprese's daughter information she might be able to use. I can't get *you* to listen to me."

Dawson paced, hoping to work off the frustration and anger he felt every time he talked to his dad these days. "All I hear is how nothing is your fault, how you've been framed." He stopped and glared at his dad. "Everybody in prison was framed."

Michael stood. He was almost as tall as Dawson and still

in pretty good shape, even though he hadn't done much since he'd gotten out of prison. "Let's go downstairs," he said. "I don't want to wake your mother."

"Right. I doubt a freight train could wake her."

Michael whirled on him, his fist raised. "You watch your mouth."

Dawson feinted and took a defensive stance, doubling his hands into fists. "What? Did I say something that isn't true?"

"You don't disrespect your mother. Not now, not ever. Do you understand?" Michael warned, advancing on him.

Dawson lifted his chin. "Disrespect goes both ways, *Dad*. You—"

"J.D.?"

He froze. So did his dad.

His mother stood in the door to the den. She was in an elegant blue satin dressing gown and her blond hair was mussed as if she'd been asleep. She held a pack of cigarettes and a jeweled lighter. Her eyes were swollen—from sleep or booze? Dawson couldn't tell.

"Mom," he said, resisting an urge to shuffle his feet like a kid.

"Edie," his dad said at the same time.

"What are you doing?" Edina Delancey asked, pushing a strand of hair back from her forehead with the hand that held the lighter.

"Just talking," Michael said. "I thought you were asleep."

She shook her head. "I couldn't sleep. I came downstairs to have a cigarette. Then I heard you two arguing." She gave Dawson an assessing glance. "Aren't you going to give me a kiss?"

Grimacing inwardly, Dawson crossed the room and bent to kiss his mother's cheek, steeling himself against the smell of gin that always clung to her like perfume.

But the only scents that hit his nose were the faint smell

of cigarette smoke and roses, which jarred him with a long-forgotten memory. Rosemary and he sitting with her on the couch while she read to them.

"I'll be downstairs," Michael said.

As his footsteps faded on the stairs, Dawson's mother touched his cheek with a trembling hand. "You shouldn't be so hard on your father, darling. He's hard enough on himself."

"How're you doing, Mom?" he asked, not wanting to get into a conversation with her about Michael.

She smiled and he saw a glint of something in her eyes that he hadn't seen in a long time. Determination. She'd started drinking heavily after his sister, Rosemary, was murdered twelve years ago. By the time Michael had gone to prison eight years ago, she'd been sober for almost a year. But Michael's sentence had been too much for her. She'd relapsed.

"One day at a time," she said, patting his cheek. "One day at a time."

Dawson smiled back at her and kissed her on the forehead before he turned to follow Michael down the stairs to the basement media room.

"J.D.—"

He turned. She'd always called him J.D. She was the only one who did. "Yeah, Mom?"

"Thank you for helping him. He had nothing to do with that tragedy. He needs you to believe in him."

Dawson clenched his jaw, but he gave his mother a small nod. "I'm going to do my best to find out the truth," he said. That was the most he could offer.

Downstairs, Michael had turned on a classical music station. He watched Dawson descend the stairs.

"Mom's sober?" Dawson asked.

Michael's mouth thinned, but he nodded. "Three weeks. She's on medication. I wish she'd quit smoking, but I guess she needs them right now."

The idea that his mom was trying to get sober planted a lump in Dawson's throat. For some reason, it upped the anger at his dad. "What she doesn't need is her husband going back to prison," he bit out.

His dad grimaced. "Son, I know you don't think much of me. I don't think much of myself sometimes, but I'm tired of trying to convince you that I didn't have anything to do with that damned Sky Walk falling."

"Who is Knoblock and why haven't I heard about him before?"

Michael sighed. "Damn it. Do you have any idea how hard it is to talk to a stubborn mule who's already made up his mind that you're guilty?"

"Do you know how hard it is to have an ex-con for a father?"

Michael's face drained of color. The two of them faced off for a brief moment, then Michael shook his head. "You should remember Knoblock. He was the concrete subcontractor on the condos."

"That was Knoblock? Thick glasses? I do remember him, barely." Dawson had worked for his dad as a framer and a roofer. By the time Michael had been indicted, Dawson had already decided that he was through with construction and his dad.

Michael nodded. "I've told you about Tito Vega, the low-life bum who got me put in prison," he said.

Dawson snorted. "Right. I know who Tito Vega is. What about him?"

"Back around the time I was bidding for the contract on the Pearl River Condominiums, I got some information from one of the building inspectors I used that Vega had another inspector in his pocket."

Dawson sat down on his dad's favorite leather couch. He absently rubbed his fingers over the worn leather on the seats.

"Come on, Dad," he said. "I've heard all this before. I've got a stack of files two feet high on Vega, but I didn't find a thing."

Michael looked at him in surprise. "You investigated Vega? For whom?"

Dawson gave him an exasperated look. "The point is, I couldn't find anything linking him to anything illegal."

"Of course you couldn't. The most you'll ever find is an op-ed piece here and there. Vega's a very smart, very careful man. And very influential. He sinks a lot of money into local politics and charities. If you've got that much information on him, you know about his real-estate business. Some of what he does is buy run-down properties, raze the buildings and put up condos or office buildings or what have you. If he has a building inspector in his pocket..." Michael spread his hands.

Dawson nodded. "So you went to the board?"

"I did what I thought was the right thing and it ended up costing me my career, my dignity and a pant load of my money." Michael wiped his face.

"The inspector who came to me knew a sucker when he saw one. He figured I'd go to the board, and he was right. He couldn't—he'd lose his job. But his real fear was Vega. He told me a few stories he'd heard." Michael shook his head. "They sounded like something out of one of Pop's stories. Threats. Dead pets. Broken legs."

Dawson stared at his dad. "How could somebody as high-profile as Vega get away with that kind of thing?" he asked.

Michael rubbed his eyes. "Pop used to say that the nation needed organized crime. He said politics and crime were like love and marriage—you know that old song. *You can't have one without the other.*"

Dawson snorted. "I'm sure that worked—for him. Come on, Dad. Talk about being in somebody's pocket, Con

Delancey was probably in the pockets of every crook in Louisiana, or vice versa."

"Your grandfather had a relationship with the top crime boss on the Gulf Coast back in the day. They were friends. They respected each other's position. Not like today. My point is that Tito Vega's got the same kind of relationship with some of the local elected officials around here. The difference is that he has no integrity. He doesn't care who he hurts. And apparently neither do the politicians."

"Integrity? Con Delancey?"

"I'm just telling you what Pop used to tell me. It was different back then. When I reported Vega for having a building inspector on his payroll, there was a big investigation, sure. But Vega managed to come out smelling like a rose." Michael paced to the sliding glass doors and back across the room to where Dawson was sitting.

"A few weeks after I won the contract for the Pearl River job, a big bald-headed goon in a thousand-dollar suit came to my office. He sat and filed his nails while he told me that I needed to hire Randall Knoblock as a subcontractor." Michael paused. "He had some kind of accent."

He looked down at Dawson. "The inspector who was in Vega's pocket was the one who reported that I'd used inferior materials on the Pearl River Condos. When the state board investigated, sure enough, the reinforced concrete on the stairs was not up to the American Concrete Institute's building code. Knoblock had disappeared, but he'd left behind files with notes that made it look like skimping on the concrete was my idea."

"And you went to prison for a crime you didn't commit," Dawson drawled. "Nice story. How come you never told me all this before?"

His dad shrugged. "You'd already tried me and found me guilty. How come you never asked me my side of it?"

Dawson didn't have an answer for that. He'd idolized his dad from the time he was old enough to understand that there was a big difference between his cousins' family and his. He and his cousin Lucas were about the same age. They and Brad Grayson, Lucas's best friend, had hung out together a lot, but not often at Lucas's house. There was always yelling and throwing things and sometimes hitting at Lucas's house.

"Whatever happened to Knoblock?"

"When I got out of prison, I had to jump through a lot of hoops, but although I couldn't get my architect's license back, I finally got my contractor license restored. I couldn't get any decent jobs, though. My reputation had been destroyed." Michael laughed harshly.

"Then an attorney from some corporation contacted me. The corporation wanted to build a casino in Waveland. They offered me a low-ball figure to take the contract. I managed to get them to raise the offer a little, but not much. I wouldn't make much, but the Golden Galaxy was the biggest casino on the Mississippi Gulf Coast, and was going to feature the Sky Walk, a unique architectural feature that would be famous around the world. I figured if it was half as successful as they were claiming, I'd be back in business."

"The corporation was Meadow Gold," Dawson said. "It belongs to Vega."

"What?" Michael stared at him.

"Juliana figured it out. She showed me a flowchart she put together that connects Meadow Gold to Tito Vega. I haven't verified all her research, but it looks like I might be able to prove he owns Meadow Gold."

Michael's gaze snapped to his. "I'll be damned."

"First, though, I've got to prove a connection between Vega and Bayside Industries. I've got one of my guys checking it out. Ever heard of them?"

Michael shook his head. "I don't think so."

"I hope Mack can find something. So you were talking about Knoblock?" Dawson pressed.

"Yeah. After I signed the contract to build the casino and had started work, I got a call from Vega. He *suggested* I subcontract the Sky Walk to Knoblock. I wanted to build that thing myself. It was going to be spectacular. Besides, Knoblock had screwed me before on the condos."

"Vega called you?"

Michael nodded. "I'm sure he used a throwaway cell. He's too smart to slip up. I told him no. I wouldn't hire Knoblock."

Dawson waited, but Michael stopped pacing and sat down in a club chair near the couch and rubbed his eyes. When he looked up, his cheeks had no color and his eyes looked haunted. He took a deep breath.

"Vega was polite. Said he understood how I felt. But the next day, the goon in the suit came to see me. He did exactly the same thing he'd done before—sat down and filed his nails. He had on an opal ring. He never even looked at me." Michael swallowed. "After he'd sat there—I swear, at least five minutes—he said, 'It's a shame about your wife. I know you'd hate it if she were driving drunk and ran off the road.'"

## Chapter Nine

Shock paralyzed Dawson. He tried to speak but his throat had seized. Finally he croaked, "He actually said that?"

He'd guessed his dad was going to tell him Vega had somehow threatened him, but he hadn't expected this.

Michael nodded and rubbed his eyes again.

"What—" Dawson had to work to swallow "—what did you do?"

His dad laughed again, not a pleasant sound. "What the hell do you think I did? Knoblock called me and I hired him."

Dawson stood and walked over to the sliding glass doors. Tito Vega had threatened his mother's life. He slammed his palm against the glass, not caring if it broke. He almost wished it would. The anger and fear were growing so fast inside him that they needed an outlet or he would burst. Anything short of bloodletting would not be enough.

"Son, calm down."

Dawson whirled, his fists clenching. "Calm down? Calm *down?* You *hired* him? You've got two sons who are cops and you just rolled over and let the bastard—" He couldn't even finish the sentence.

Michael leveled a gaze at him. "That's right, I did. Do you think I'd take the smallest chance that your mother might be hurt?"

The question slammed Dawson in the gut. He felt about

two inches high. "No, but you could have come to one of us. You could have come to me."

His father smiled sadly. "I tend to forget how young you are."

"Young? What the hell? Are you saying I couldn't handle Vega?"

"Don't raise your voice at me!" Michael shot back. "This is what I'm talking about. You'd go off half-cocked and probably make things worse."

"At least I'd do something," Dawson shouted. "You're just a—"

"J.D.? Michael?"

It was his mother. Dawson gulped down the words he was about to fling.

Michael shot him a glare and stepped over to the stairs. "It's okay, hon. Sorry if we woke you."

Dawson heard his mother's soft footsteps on the stairs. He looked up to see her blue slippers and the blue satin robe.

"Go on back to bed," his dad said gently. "We were just having a discussion."

Edie Delancey walked down the stairs as if she were making an entrance on a Las Vegas stage. She looked at Dawson, her eyes narrowed, then turned to her husband.

"Michael, you're tired. You go on up to bed. I'll see J.D. out."

"Edie—"

"Go on, Michael."

There was a note in his mother's voice that Dawson hadn't heard in a long, long time. It reminded him that she had been a beautiful, vibrant and strong woman who had reared her children with a gentle, yet firm, hand. She'd rarely raised her voice, but all the kids knew that when they heard that tone, they'd better obey.

He shook his head, trying to rid himself of the conflicting emotions churning inside him.

Once Michael's footsteps got to the top of the stairs and faded away on the hardwood floors, Edie turned to her son.

"Mom," Dawson said in a futile attempt to stave off whatever she was going to say, which he knew would add shame and more guilt to the mix of feelings inside him.

"I know what your father has been telling you."

"Look, Mom, it's just a business thing—"

"No," she said, holding up a slender hand. "No, it's not. I know, J.D.," she said. "I *know*."

"You know?" He tried one more time to pretend he didn't understand her. "About what?"

Her mouth turned up in a small smile, another reminder of what a beautiful woman she was.

"About everything," she said patiently. "The threats. The demands."

He had nothing to say. He couldn't tell her she was wrong. She knew she wasn't. He couldn't tell her the threats were nothing because they weren't nothing. He'd seen in his dad's face, heard in his voice, that the deadly threat was real. If his dad hadn't complied with Vega's demands, his mother might well have died.

"Your father needs you. He needs you to believe in him." She stepped closer to him and laid her hand on his chest, over his heart. "You know, in here, that he wouldn't skimp on materials."

Dawson took an instinctive step backward. His mother was acting too much like her old self and it was messing with his brain. And his heart. She'd always been able to see through him.

"I don't know that," he protested. "Look at Grampa. He screwed people for a living and they still voted for him every election. Look at Uncle Robert. He's like Con reincarnated.

I used to hear him yelling and hitting stuff—sometimes hitting Aunt Bettye or the kids."

His mother's delicate brows lowered. "What are you saying?"

His gaze lit on the glass door. In the dim light he could see his palm print on the glass. "What makes my dad different from his brother or his own father?" He looked down at his palm.

"And what makes me different from any of them?" Hearing the words that he'd never said, even to himself, stunned him.

"You think you're like your grandfather or your uncle? You think your father is like them?" Edie shook her head. "No. Michael is not and you're not."

"Mom, I just nearly put my hand through the glass door over there," Dawson protested, feeling his face heat up. "I don't like knowing I can do that."

"You listen to me, John Dawson Delancey," she said. "Your father went into construction because he wanted to get as far away from politics as he could. He wanted to make his own legacy. He was never more proud than when you went to work with him. Knowing that you believed he was guilty hurt him much more than even going to prison."

Dawson walked over to the glass doors and looked out. It was pitch-black outside, but he couldn't face his mother right then. He swallowed against the huge lump that had grown in his throat. "You believe he was innocent?" he asked, his voice hoarse.

"Of course I do," she said. "I believe in him."

"I can't—" Dawson swallowed again and rubbed his eyes. "I just don't know."

"J.D., look at me."

He looked down at his feet, then took a deep breath and turned around.

"I need you to do something for me."

He grimaced. "Mom—"

"Don't interrupt your mother. Even if you don't believe your father, even if you don't believe me, I need you to do everything you can to prove what really happened to the Sky Walk."

Dawson nodded. "I am, Mom. I'm going to uncover the truth, no matter what it is."

"That's all you can do, darling," she said. "Now, it's late. Why don't you stay here in your old room instead of driving all the way back to your condo?"

Dawson looked at his watch. It was eleven o'clock. "I can't. I've got to get back. Jules is there by herself—" He stopped but not soon enough.

"Jules?" his mother echoed. "Who is Jules? I didn't know you were dating someone."

"Trust me," he said, "I am *not* dating her. She's Juliana Caprese. She's the daughter of the casino manager who was killed when the Sky Walk collapsed."

"Oh, the poor girl. How awful for her."

He nodded. "Yeah. Okay, well, I need to go—"

"If you're not dating, what's she doing at your condo? Is she in some kind of protective custody?"

"No. Well, kind of." He moved toward the stairs.

"J.D.," Edie said, propping her fists on her hips. "What's going on with you and that girl?"

He laughed. "Okay, Mom. First, I'm thirty-two, not sixteen, okay?" He sighed. "Someone's been following her, so she's staying at my place."

"Following her? Why?"

"She's been looking into her father's death," Dawson said. "We're working together to figure out why the Sky Walk fell."

Edie frowned at him. "That seems odd," she said thoughtfully. "If her father was killed when the Sky Walk collapsed, and *your* father is being investigated because it collapsed, why would she want to work with you?"

He felt his face heat up again.

"Oh, my," his mother said. "She doesn't know that you're Michael Delancey's son, does she?"

ALL THE WAY BACK TO HIS CONDO, his mother's words echoed in his ears.

*She doesn't know you're Michael Delancey's son.* He'd planned it that way, of course, but hearing the words in his mom's disappointed voice made his brilliant idea seem more sleazy than smart.

He saw the lights on in the living room. He really hoped she'd left them on when she went to bed because he didn't feel like facing her with his mom's accusing voice still echoing in his ears.

She was tucked into the corner of his leather couch, with one of her manila folders open on her lap. Beside her was her gun. She looked up. Was that relief on her face? Had she really been scared to stay by herself?

"Hey, I thought you were going to bed," he said. "I smell popcorn."

She nodded toward the coffee table. "There's about half of it left if you want it. It's extra-buttery."

He didn't want popcorn. "I know. I bought it."

She stretched her legs. She had on a pink tank top that said Pink on it and pink-and-gray plaid pajama bottoms that stopped right below her knees. Her calves were smooth and shapely. He could see the edge of a strip bandage on her left knee. It didn't completely cover the scrape from her attack.

When his gaze slid down to her slender ankles and bare feet, his mouth went dry. Those toes. Pink-tipped and sexy. Struggling to swallow, he pulled his gaze back up to her face.

She closed the folder and set it on top of the others on the coffee table, then lifted her gaze to his. She blinked and her tongue flicked out to moisten her lips.

Dawson nearly groaned aloud at the sudden exquisite ache in his groin. If he didn't get a grip she'd soon know exactly how badly he wanted her. Not just for sex. He'd decided a few years ago that sex for sex's sake was an exercise in frustration and boredom. It served its purpose, but he preferred women who could keep up with him other than just between the sheets. And he'd never met anyone as beautiful, as smart or as fascinating as Juliana Caprese. From those dark, snapping eyes to her sexy pink toes, she embodied the perfect woman. As the thought slid through his mind, he saw her breasts tighten under the thin pink top. Adrenaline pumped pure lust through him.

Her eyes narrowed, she lifted her chin and he crashed back into the real world. Which was a good thing, because once she found out who he was, she'd send him crashing to hell if she could.

"How was your appointment?" she said frostily.

"Appointment?" For a split second, he was confused. "Oh, right. It was fine. Lasted longer than I'd hoped it would."

She assessed him for a full three seconds, then nodded and picked up the folders. "Well, if you're going to be a private eye," she said casually as she stood, "you have to be available when your client needs you."

Dawson chuckled.

She wrapped her arms around the folders. Her teeth grazed her lower lip. "What if I need you?" she asked.

Dawson's chuckle dissolved. What the hell? "I'm right here," he said softly. "What do you need?"

She shook her head. "I was scared while you were gone."

He stiffened, looking at her gun on the couch. "Did something happen?"

"No, but—"

He stepped closer until her arms, wrapped around the folders brushed against his shirt. "I thought you said you could handle that weapon."

She shrugged, and Dawson couldn't take his eyes off the bony, sexy curve of her shoulder. Her skin was beautiful, a kind of a ripe-peach color that made his mouth water.

He slid his fingers along the slope of her neck down to her shoulder. He touched the little bump that defined the shoulder socket.

Juliana shivered and raised her gaze to meet Dawson's intense blue eyes. What was it about him that made all rational thought fly out of her head? Silly question. It was everything about him. Starting with his hands. Those large, beautiful hands that she knew would be able to stir her into a frenzy within seconds. Then there were his eyes—no matter how cocky and sarcastic he was, she'd found out that if she was quick enough, she could see a bit of the truth in them. Right now those intense blue lasers were promising her delights that she'd never before experienced.

His mouth was curved, not sarcastically, but gently, sensually. She looked at it, imagining how he would use it. Which was a mistake, because she'd always had a vivid imagination. A tiny moan gathered deep in her throat.

Dawson bent his head and touched her lips with his. At the feel of his mouth, her lips parted and Pandora's box opened deep inside her, releasing a cloud of confusing, conflicting emotions. It had cracked open a little in her dad's office the last time he'd kissed her.

But here there were no deadly beams to crash down on them. Here, the only danger was to her heart. And while he'd been her savior then, now he was the danger.

He wrapped an arm around her and pulled her to him, crushing the folders between them.

She stiffened automatically.

Dawson pulled back and stared down at her. He grabbed the folders and tugged on them. "Still don't trust me, do you?"

"No," she gasped, forcing herself to let go of them. "I mean— I didn't mean to—"

"It's okay," he said, his jaw clenching. "I shouldn't have—"

"Put them down," she said.

"What?" His jaw muscle worked. "Hey, Jules, come on—"

"Put them down—over there." She pointed to the couch. "On the floor, anywhere. I don't care." Then she moved, pressing her body against him, and kissed the line of his jaw. "And relax," she whispered, running a finger along his jawline.

Dawson tossed them onto an end table and pulled her close until she could feel the hardness of his erection against her. He pressed her closer, moving his hips in slow, rhythmic motion as he kissed her.

The pulsing rhythm sent electricity arcing through her as his mouth explored hers. His tongue slid along her lower lip, tickling, teasing, before it delved inside, pushing past her teeth and flirting with her tongue.

Sensation swept her up into a whirlwind. Nothing existed except her body and Dawson's, molded together, heat melding with heat, motion echoing motion.

Somehow, while she was flying inside the whirlwind, they were magically transported to his bed. Her pajamas were gone. He threw off his jeans and shirt and lay down beside her. His body was hot and firm and smooth, and he was engorged—so ready for her that it was a little scary.

But he was in no hurry. His hands explored her body, caressing her, massaging her, delving into secret folds and finding erogenous zones that she had no idea existed.

She did her best to give back as good as she got, but he

was relentless, and she kept forgetting everything except her own pleasure.

That didn't seem to bother him. After he'd brought her to climax with his fingers, he let his mouth do the exploring, and stirred her to a peak even higher than before.

"Dawson," she gasped. "Please." She grasped at his shoulders, pulling him to her. He took his time traveling up her body, stopping to nip and suck at her breasts until she was panting.

He lifted himself above her and kissed her, leaving his own taste in her mouth. Every tendon in her body contracted in an erotic electrical storm as he entered her smoothly and deeply.

Surging and crashing like an ocean wave, she lost all control for the first time in her life. When the waves finally waned, she collapsed, as scattered and still as the sand.

Dawson buried his head in Juliana's neck and waited for his breathing to return to normal. He'd never lost control like that in his life.

He'd planned to stoke her slowly and deliberately, coaxing her to the most explosive orgasm she'd ever had. In fact, if she held on to everything as tightly as she held on to those folders, he wouldn't be surprised if she'd never had one.

But he'd been hoisted by his own petard. Not only had she exploded for the third time as soon as he'd entered her, her explosion had triggered his own. He shuddered as tiny aftershocks sparked and fired through him.

She trailed her fingers down his back, sending goose bumps across his skin. He lifted his head and smiled at her. Her eyes drifted open and she peered at him through thick black lashes. Her teeth scraped across her bottom lip and she smiled back at him.

He felt a twinge deep inside him at the sight of that shy smile. It was oddly painful—and uncomfortably familiar.

Suddenly he needed to separate himself from her. So he bussed the tip of her nose, then rolled away and threw his arm over his eyes.

"Dawson, are you okay?" she asked.

"Sure." He hoped his arm hid his grimace. He wasn't okay, but he didn't want to talk about it. The twinge he'd felt was the same queasy feeling he'd gotten while talking to his mom.

How had all those things he'd never even consciously thought to himself come bubbling out as soon as his dad had left the room? He'd never dwelled on his family's scandalous legacy—other than to joke about it to family and friends. It had surprised him how much he did not want to be like his grandfather or his abusive uncle Robert.

It was admirable that his mother thought his dad was a good man who'd been framed for a crime he hadn't committed. But Dawson wasn't so sure.

*Not sure.* A week ago he'd been positive his dad was guilty. How had his mom managed to plant doubt in his mind? What had changed?

As soon as the question hit his brain, he knew the answer.

*Juliana.* Once he'd met her, everything changed. Listening to her accuse Michael of killing her father had shaken his certainty. Suddenly, he found himself defending his dad.

And now he'd screwed up royally. He'd known before he'd walked in that he didn't want to talk to her tonight. Didn't want to see her. His subconscious, knowing how vulnerable he was after talking with his mom, had been trying to protect him.

It hadn't helped that Juliana had thrown herself at him. *No.* That wasn't fair to her. When she'd said she needed him, all she'd meant was that she'd been afraid to be by herself. He was the one who'd taken it to the next level.

A thrill—half lustful, half fearful—swirled through him.

The next level and the next and the next. He was still stunned by the intensity of his orgasm—of his and hers.

He lowered his arm and when he did, Juliana turned and laid her head on his shoulder. Her breathing turned soft and even. She was asleep.

Dawson shifted into a more comfortable position and closed his eyes. He breathed deeply, filling his head with the scent of peppermint from her hair.

As he drifted off, it occurred to him that this was the first time a woman had slept in his bed since—when?

Since ever.

# Chapter Ten

Dawson woke up with a start. Something wasn't right. He opened his eyes and saw a cloud of soft black hair draped across his arm.

Juliana was in his bed with him. It was five-thirty in the morning. Ugh. A part of him wanted to turn over, snuggle up against her naked body and wake her with foreplay. But when he looked at her, peacefully sleeping, trusting him to keep her safe, guilt racked him. He was lying to her. Not just with words, but with everything he did, every move he made. She had no idea who he was.

If—when she found out, she would brand him with the same label he'd used on his grandfather, his uncle and even his dad. And he would deserve it as much as they did—possibly more than his dad did.

He slid out of bed, grabbed a pair of underwear and his favorite around-the-house jeans and slipped out of the bedroom, easing the door closed behind him. He headed to the bathroom, yawning and stretching.

After a fast hot shower, he made coffee and paced in front of his living-room window as he drank it. What was he going to say—what was he going to do—when she woke up?

Would she be battling the same mixed emotions he was? He seriously doubted she slept around. Not as tightly as she held on to those folders.

The folders. He turned and looked at them, stacked on the coffee table. He glanced toward the bedroom and back again. He was dying to look at them. He couldn't imagine that she had much that he didn't already know. But she was sharp and thorough.

He thought about the flowchart she'd put together of the corporations Tito Vega was connected with. The work she'd put into making all those connections was a testament to her determination and focus. It would be interesting to know if any of the city officials and charitable organizations that courted Vega's money for their pet projects knew about all of Vega's involvements.

Glancing at his watch, he wondered what Mack was doing right now. In Zurich it would be—he did the math in his head—around one o'clock today: Saturday. He didn't know what flight Mack had been able to catch. Had he had time to see his little secretary last night? He sighed. He probably wouldn't hear a word until Sunday or even Monday.

He sat down on the couch and set his coffee cup aside. Damn, he wanted to get his hands on those folders—had ever since he'd first seen them.

Did he dare?

*If you want to be a private eye, you can't be squeamish about snooping into other people's stuff.* He smiled to himself.

He had to admit it was fun to tease Juliana about wanting to be a private investigator. An unexpected and disturbing vision rose in his mind—of the two of them working together, his handling the legwork and her working on the research and paperwork he found so tedious. The disturbing part of his little daydream was that when the day was over, they went home together.

All right, damn it. He rubbed his eyes. What was he going

to do? He glanced toward the bedroom, wondering how late she slept.

He growled. He needed to listen to his own rules about being a private eye. He reached for the top folder, the one she'd been looking at when he'd come in. The tab was labeled Knoblock.

Dawson's pulse sped up. She had information on Knoblock. Hadn't he asked her if she'd heard the name Knoblock? She said she wasn't sure.

She'd lied to him.

He opened the folder. On top of the thin stack of papers was a building permit filed by Randall Knoblock for the Sky Walk inside the Golden Galaxy. He had listed himself as a subcontractor working under Michael Delancey.

Dawson shook his head. He had to admit it wasn't a stretch for Juliana to assume that Michael had not only been responsible for what Knoblock did on the Sky Walk, but that he'd ordered it.

Hell, that's what he'd thought himself—at first.

The sheet under the building permit was a copy of a newspaper article listing indictments. A date, May 23, 1997, was handwritten as was the name of the newspaper, the *Kansas City Star*. The charges listed by Knoblock's name included criminal negligence. Dawson cursed under his breath. Apparently, Knoblock had made a long and obviously successful career of skimping on materials.

How had Jules tracked down all this information? As far as Dawson knew there wasn't a centralized database of crooked contractors. He was impressed.

Dawson set that sheet aside and looked at the next one. It was a copy of a three-line piece that stated that on April 10, 2000, Randall Knoblock was released from prison.

Just as Dawson picked it up, he saw a movement out of the corner of his eye.

"What are you doing?" Juliana stood in the doorway to the living room in her pink pajamas. Her hair was tangled and her eyes were heavy-lidded.

"Jules—" he said defensively, setting the folder down and standing.

"Don't call me that," she snapped. "What are you doing with my folders?"

"I just wanted to take a look at them—" Dawson started.

"You have no right. Those are mine! I did *not* give you permission to look at them."

Her anger was way out of proportion, he thought. "Come on, Jules. I only looked at one folder, Knoblock's. It's not like we haven't already talked about him. Think about my—about the note. *It* mentioned him. In fact, I asked you specifically if you knew the name and you said you weren't sure."

She glared at him and pushed her hands through her hair, pulling it back and twisting it up.

"You shouldn't be snooping," she said, much less vehemently.

"Hey," he said, spreading his hands. "If you want my help, you're going to have to trust me."

The look on her face gave him the answer to the question he'd asked himself earlier. Her cheeks were pink and she wouldn't meet his gaze. Obviously, she'd decided that sex with him had been a mistake. Well, she could join the club.

"Look," he said placatingly, "I can see that you're thinking the same thing I am. So I'll make a promise to you right now. I swear to you that *that*—" he nodded toward the bedroom "—won't happen again. Okay? How's that? Because if we can't trust each other, then neither one of us is going to get what we want."

Her cheeks flamed even brighter than before. "It won't happen again?" she whispered.

Dawson grimaced. He hated that her voice was so small

and tentative. It was a blow to his ego that she regretted making love with him that much.

"No, it won't," he said, but couldn't resist adding, "unless you want it to." He shrugged and smiled.

She didn't smile back. "I have to—" she cocked her head slightly backward "—to take a shower." She turned on her heel and disappeared. He heard the door to the guest room close, then open a few seconds later. Then he heard the bathroom door close.

He blew out a long breath. "Way to go, Delancey," he growled.

JULIANA LIFTED HER FACE to the hot spray, pretending that the wetness on her face was a hundred percent water and zero percent tears, and that the heat was the steam rather than embarrassment and humiliation.

*That won't happen again.* Dawson's emphatic declaration had sent hurt and embarrassment stabbing through her. She'd woken up in his bed, stretching languidly, satiated after a night of lovemaking that could only be described as mind-blowing, to find that his side of the bed was empty and cold.

*Uh-oh,* her little voice said. *Are things going to be awkward?* Dawson probably brought women to his apartment all the time. If she judged by his looks, personality and performance in bed, she'd have to conclude that he got a *lot* of practice.

She, on the other hand, did not. She got offers and come-ons, but she was very picky about who she went to bed with. The trail of lovers she'd left in her wake was extremely short—practically nonexistent, in fact. Two hardly qualified as a trail.

She turned around to let the hot water run on her back as she remembered his hot, hard body against hers. She didn't know what made his touch different, but as soon as he'd caressed her, all the careful control she brought to everything had dissolved.

When she thought about how abandoned, maybe even wanton, she'd been, her face burned again. She'd done things, and so had he, that she'd never experienced before.

An aftershock of pleasure centered in her core, turning her knees to jelly. She moaned and steadied herself with a hand against the shower wall as she arched in reaction and tears welled in her eyes. To have a climax, even a tiny one, by just thinking about what they'd done—nothing like that had ever happened to her, either.

And never would again. To her dismay, she was crying again. She had to get a grip. She couldn't let Dawson know how much he'd hurt her. She'd just have to act as though she was as blasé about the sex as he was. It's probably what he was used to—given the type of women she imagined him dating.

She shivered. The shower water was cooling off. She quickly bathed and washed her hair, then grabbed a towel. As she dried off, she thought about him sneaking a look at her folders.

Anger swept through her—at him for snooping. At herself for hanging on to those few pages of information she'd unearthed. She ran her fingers through her wet hair, then dried off the mirror and looked at herself.

Her eyes grew wide and her mouth fell open as a disturbing thought occurred to her. Dawson had come to her. He'd been the one to suggest that they work together. And he'd been eyeing those folders from the beginning.

Juliana didn't like what her brain was telling her, but it made sense. Pitiful sense. She knew that whatever tiny bits of information she'd gleaned needed to be shared with Dawson if they were going to ever figure out what had happened to the Sky Walk. But she'd clung to those folders—not because they contained valuable information she didn't want Dawson to have, but because they *didn't*.

As soon as Dawson realized how little information she had, he'd realize he didn't need her a quarter as much as she needed him. And then he'd be gone.

A brisk knock sounded on the door, startling her. "Jules, I just got a call from Brian—Detective Hardy. They've got a match for the fingerprints they lifted off the beam. The guy's in custody, and they want us down there."

She frowned at herself in the mirror. "But we didn't see anybody."

"Just hurry up," he snapped.

She winced at the tone in his voice. "Do I have time to dry my hair?" she called out, but she heard his footsteps walking away.

She towel dried her hair and rushed to pull on jeans and a top. Obviously, there was no time to put on makeup or fix her hair. So she caught her damp waves up in a ponytail, grabbed her purse and headed to the kitchen.

Dawson was waiting, jingling his car keys. When he saw her his brows drew down for an instant, but he didn't say a word. He just opened the door to the garage and stood back for her to precede him down the stairs.

AT THE POLICE STATION, which was nearly vacant because it was Saturday, Dawson glanced around. He saw Brian Hardy coming out of what must have been the break room, carrying a steaming cup of coffee. He saw them and walked over.

"Morning, Dawson, Ms. Caprese. Coffee?"

Dawson shook his head.

Jules leaned forward and sniffed near Brian's coffee cup. "Yes, please, if it's even half as good as it smells."

Brian smiled at her. "Maybe half as good, if you're lucky. How do you take it?"

"Black is fine."

"I'll be right back."

Once the detective had walked away, Dawson said, "While we're here, I want to ask Brian if he knows anything about Randall Knoblock."

Jules looked at him with a frown. "Go ahead," she said.

He clenched his jaw. "I don't want to step on your toes, seeing how upset you were that I looked at your little folder."

He was being mean and he knew it, but it frustrated the hell out of him that she didn't trust him enough to share with him information that could help to figure out who had caused the Sky Walk to collapse. He wanted to tell her that there was nothing in her precious folders that he couldn't find out on his own, given enough time. He wanted to point out to her that the whole concept of *working together* meant sharing information.

Jules shot him a glare. "Like you said, we'd already talked about Knoblock."

His brows shot up. What was that? A semiapology for being so possessive about her folders?

Brian came back with a second steaming cup of coffee. "The suspect is in the interrogation room. His name is William Maynard. I'm going to take you two into the viewing room, where you can see him through the one-way mirror. See if you recognize him."

"I don't understand," Jules said. "I didn't see anybody and I don't think Dawson did, either."

"I don't remember seeing anyone," Dawson agreed. "But it's amazing what your subconscious notices—someone walking on the street or sitting in a car. It doesn't register at the time, but if you see them again, like this—" he gestured toward the interrogation room "—you might remember."

The detective led the way to the viewing room, which was dark as pitch. He flipped on a light switch, and the glass panel on the wall revealed a skinny guy fidgeting in a wooden chair. He had on a black T-shirt and his arms and neck were covered with tattoos. He was facing the one-way glass. When Brian closed the door, he looked up.

"He can't see us, right? Can he hear us?" Jules whispered.

Dawson shook his head as Brian answered. "Nope. He might have heard the door close, but he can't hear us. This room is soundproof. He sees a mirror. But he's been around enough to know that we're in here watching him."

Jules was staring through the glass with a frown on her face. "His fingerprints were on the beam that fell on us?" she asked.

"Right," Hardy said. "Why? Do you recognize him?"

"No, I don't think so. How could he have dropped that steel beam by himself? It was huge."

"I wondered that myself," Hardy answered. "He's worked construction in the past. In fact, he signed on to work on the Golden Galaxy, but he never got a paycheck. To answer your question, our genius in there dropped the bolt cutters he used to shear the bolts that held the beam. My crime scene investigator found them lying in the office area near the beam."

"Genius is right." Dawson laughed. "What's the charge— assault with intent?"

"He'll probably deal it out, but it should be worth a couple of years."

"So his fingerprints prove he dropped the beam, right?" Juliana asked. "What do you need from me?"

"It would be better if we had an eyewitness who could put him there at the right time."

"I can't do that. I did hear noises, but nothing that would prove anything." She spread her hands in a helpless gesture.

Brian glanced at Dawson. "What about the guy? Any chance you might have seen him somewhere else?"

Jules glanced narrowly from Brian to Dawson. "Somewhere else?"

She looked back at the tattooed man. Dawson followed her gaze. The little skunk was picking his teeth with a fingernail. Both teeth and nails were mottled and broken. *Crack addict.*

Jules said, "You think he's the one who stole my letter, don't you?"

"I didn't say that," Brian replied. "I was just thinking you might have spotted him somewhere if he's been following you."

Jules met Dawson's gaze. Her look said, *I know that's what he means.*

"Well?" he asked. "What do you think? Ever see him before?"

She unconsciously arched her shoulder and put a hand to the fading bruise on her face. She didn't say anything, just stared at the man.

"Talk about what you remember from the attack," Brian suggested. "Try to picture what you saw, what you felt."

She nodded, not taking her eyes off the suspect. "I walked out of the post office. I don't know where he was—not in the building. There was no one else in there." She took a breath. "I hadn't taken three steps on the sidewalk when I was hit from behind." She stopped and shook her head.

"No, not hit. Shoved. He shoved me." She nodded. "I fell on my knee, but for some reason I kept falling. I think he may have shoved me again because I landed on my shoulder— hard." She arched it again, wincing.

Dawson watched her carefully. When she didn't say anything else, he prompted her. "When did he grab the letter?"

She closed her eyes. "I had it in my hand. I don't think I realized right away that someone had hit me. My shoulder was hurting badly, but I tried to get up. That's when he—" She gasped and her eyes flew open.

# If you love THIS book...

**We'll send you 2 FREE BOOKS** from the same series right to your door when you return the attached card.

**No purchase required.** This is a fast, fun way for you to try the convenience of the Reader Service without risking a penny. Keep your free gifts with our compliments, whether or not you continue.

**Your choice of Regular or Larger Print!** Be sure to indicate whether you prefer Regular Print or Larger-Print books with 20% bigger type.

## 4 Mail card for FREE GIFTS!

# How do you spell EASY?

**E** for "**enjoy** the convenience of home delivery!"

**A** for "**absolutely** no commitment." (Try it risk-free!)

**S** for "**savings** on every book, every time!"

**Y** for "**YES!** Send me 4 FREE GIFTS worth over $20.00!"

**W**e'll send the best new books in this series *right to your door*—starting with **2 FREE BOOKS** and **2 MYSTERY GIFTS**, and no obligation to purchase anything. See details on back of this card.

See the larger-print difference. Harlequin Intrigue® books come in a larger-print format. You get the complete, unabridged book but with 20% larger type, so it's easy on your eyes!

☐ I prefer the regular-print edition
182/382 HDL FNSR

☐ I prefer the larger-print edition
199/399 HDL FNSR

FIRST NAME                    LAST NAME

ADDRESS

APT #            CITY

STATE/PROV.    ZIP/POSTAL CODE

Visit us online at
www.ReaderService.com

► DETACH AND MAIL CARD TODAY! ►

HI-RSA-05/12

## The Reader Service - Here's How It Works:

"Omigosh, that's him!" she cried. "That's him. Look at the tattoos."

"Tell me about them. Why are you so sure this is the guy?" Brian asked, his voice level.

Jules pointed.

Maynard rested his elbows on the table and was playing with a sandwich wrapper. His full sleeves of tattoos were clearly visible. "See the one on his left arm? It looks like a vine—" She paused. "Or is it a snake? Anyhow, it's got all those colors in it. He reached around me and jerked the letter out of my hand and that's what I saw. That—" She made a winding motion with her hand.

Brian set his foam cup on the table. "Great. That gives me probable cause for a warrant to search his house and car for the letter." He glanced at his watch. "I need to call Maura. Maura Presley, the A.D.A. With any luck, she can find us a judge."

"What else do you need from us?" Dawson asked.

"Just a signed statement from you," he told Juliana. "You'll need to go into detail about where and when you saw him, describe exactly what happened, step by step if you can. And state how you're positive he's the man who attacked you." Brian paused. "*If* you are. Please just state the facts. Don't get into conjecture. I need this to be as clean as possible."

Jules nodded. "What will you do? Question him? Will I need to talk to him?"

"No, no," Brian assured her. "I doubt seriously this will go to trial. Our friend in there has priors. He'll be anxious to plead this out. Maybe we can deal with him to give us whoever sicced him on you."

Jules met Dawson's gaze. He knew exactly what she was thinking. When the slimy little skunk gave up the person who'd sent him to spy on her and steal any answers she got to her newspaper ad, the name would be Michael Delancey.

While Jules wrote out her statement, Dawson talked to Brian about Randall Knoblock and got him to print out a copy of Maynard's mug shot. Then he gave Ryker a call to see if he had time to talk this afternoon. Ryker and his wife, Nicole, were painting the house they'd bought. He gave Dawson the new address.

Ten minutes later he and Jules were back in the car. She settled back against the seat with a sigh. "Did you hear that? He *was* the guy who attacked me."

"I was standing right there," he said with a smile.

"Did you talk to Detective Hardy about Knoblock?"

Dawson nodded. "He knew a little about him, mostly from the information they have on the Golden Galaxy—that he was the subcontractor for the Sky Walk." He glanced at her sidelong. "Interestingly, Hardy didn't have the information from Kansas City."

She lit up at that, just like he knew she would. She'd found something a police detective hadn't found. "Really? Did you tell him what I'd found?"

He shook his head. "I thought I'd wait and make sure you wanted to share that with him."

"Why wouldn't I," she snapped, "if it will help him figure out who's responsible for my dad's death?"

"Hey, calm down. It's Saturday and he's still got to get a warrant to search Maynard's property before some buddy of his goes in and cleans everything up."

"Maynard. He's a creepy-looking guy."

"He's a petty thief, a crack addict, a bully and a skunk. Likes to carry around a billy club."

"A billy club?" Juliana's hand went to her shoulder. "That must be what he hit me with."

"Yeah, no." He laughed harshly. "If he had, your shoulder wouldn't have been dislocated. It would have been crushed. He must have had orders not to hurt you."

"Orders from whom?" she asked with a shiver. "When will Detective Hardy know something?"

"I doubt we'll hear anything until Monday. We'll take him the information about Knoblock in Kansas City and see what he's found out."

"Great. I'm ready for all this to be over."

Dawson glanced at her. Her chin had that little pugnacious lift to it that told him she'd made up her mind about something.

"Take me to my apartment," she said.

"No, you—"

"Dawson, I need clothes. I need to get my mail, and I want my car."

"What about your shoulder?" he asked, knowing he was going to lose this fight.

"It's fine. The worst of the soreness is gone. I probably could have been driving all along."

Dawson racked his brain for a reason to refuse. He didn't want her driving. She'd go running off again and get into trouble or get herself killed. A sinking feeling hit his gut at that thought.

But if he objected, that chin would go even higher. He sighed. "I will if you'll promise me that you won't go running off without me."

She glanced sidelong at him, a veiled look that he couldn't interpret. "Why would I do that?" she asked. "We're working together, right?"

A sense of foreboding settled on Dawson's chest. He wanted to lock her away like Rapunzel or another of those fairy-tale princesses. But the princesses always managed to get into trouble anyway, and he was sure Jules would, too. "Right," he said wryly.

## Chapter Eleven

Juliana drove to Dawson's condo after taking care of some chores and washing some clothes. She parked on the street and knocked on the front door.

When he opened it, he was talking on the phone.

"Right," he said as she walked past him. "I'll have to go to the office and check the files. I'll call you from there."

She waited until he hung up, then said, "I still don't see why I can't stay at my own place."

Dawson pocketed his phone and checked his watch before he raised his gaze to hers.

"After two attacks, you're not convinced you're in danger? I'd think you'd be glad I'm keeping an eye on you. I just don't want to be responsible for scraping you up off the floor."

"First, thanks for that image. Second, nobody asked you to be responsible for me. And third, now that Maynard guy is locked up, how am I still in danger?" She walked into the living room while she was talking. The folders on the coffee table were still stacked neatly with the top one slightly crooked, just like she'd left them.

She grimaced to herself. Somehow she had to work up the courage to share her meager information with Dawson. If he took it and ran, wasn't she still better off than if she hadn't confided in him at all? He'd helped her get her dad's things from the casino. He'd saved her life.

"Damn it, Jules. If you're going to be a private eye—hell, if you're going to *survive*—you're going to have to stop being so stubborn and start using your brain for something more than getting the last word." He blew out a breath in frustration. "Why don't you think about it for a few seconds and tell me how you can still be in danger."

Juliana spoke through gritted teeth. "Okay, okay. I know. Because Maynard may be in custody, but whoever hired him is still out there."

"And…"

She frowned. "And…"

"Maynard will make bail before morning."

"They'll give him bail—after he attacked me?"

Dawson sighed. "Don't you watch any of the cop shows on TV?"

"Stop it. You don't have to be so sarcastic all the time." She tossed her purse down on the couch and looked at the folders again, taking a deep breath. "Dawson—"

"Don't worry, Jules, I haven't touched them."

She turned. "I know. I—" She swallowed. Why was this so hard? "If you want, we could look at them together."

Dawson's brows shot up and an unreadable expression crossed his face. He stared at her for an instant, then turned and picked up his keys off the table by the door.

"Maybe later," he said. "Right now there's something I've got to do."

"About the casino? Can I go with you?"

"No. Believe it or not, I have other cases. I'll be back as soon as I can."

"You said you're going to your office. I want to see a real private investigations office."

"It's a security agency, and no." He pointed at her with the hand that held the keys. "Don't leave."

"And keep the door locked," she said mockingly.

That earned her a fierce scowl. His laser-blue eyes nearly scorched her. "If I had half a brain I'd get Brian to put you in jail for your own safety," he growled, then stalked up the hall to the kitchen and out the door to the garage.

Juliana let out a quiet, frustrated scream and stomped her foot. He made her so mad! She balled her fists and punched the air in front of her.

Then she stomped into the guest bedroom and jerked the band out of her hair and pushed her fingers through it. Meeting her own gaze in the mirror over the dresser, she shook her head until her hair stood out like Medusa's snakes. She grabbed a comb and worked out her anger and frustration while she worked the snarls out of her hair.

By the time her hair was smooth, she'd stopped fuming and was thinking relatively rationally.

Before Dawson had driven all reason out of her head last night, before Detective Hardy had called her in to identify Maynard, she'd thought of something she'd wanted to do. What was it?

She walked up the hall to the kitchen to get some water. She brought the glass into the living room and set it on the coffee table next to the stack of folders.

Looking at them stoked her anger again. She'd made what she considered a huge concession, offering to let Dawson look at her stack of research, which contained every bit of information she'd managed to gather about everyone connected with the Sky Walk. But after all his curiosity, all his staring at them, he'd brushed off her offer as if it was nothing. He didn't have time. He had something he had to do. *Another matter.*

Juliana flopped down on the couch. She drank the cool water and tried to clear her brain.

*Everyone connected with the Sky Walk.* Something—some name—was bothering her. She closed her eyes and tried to concentrate. She picked up her folders and looked at the tabs. *Delancey. Knoblock. Vega. Kaplan.*

A thought tickled the back of her brain, teasing her. Looking at the four names didn't help. Everybody knew the name Delancey. The Delancey family had been prominent in Louisiana politics for years. For that matter, Vega was a well-known name along the coast. The other names weren't familiar.

She stared at the names, trying to make one of them fit her recollection. She couldn't. What name was it that was bothering her? Someone her dad had mentioned? No. The sense she had was of an old memory—school maybe? But when? Where? College? High school? *Grade school?*

Her suitcase was still standing just inside the door. She opened it and dug out her mini-notebook computer. Back on the couch, she looked up her high school. There was no list of alumni on the site. She tried some social networking sites, but although she found several people she knew, not one of their names scratched the itch in the back of her brain.

Nor did she find a complete list of the members of her graduating class anywhere.

She turned off the computer and stood. There was a better way. She grabbed her car keys, then realized she didn't have a key to Dawson's condo. After looking in a few obvious places and coming up empty, she left him a note telling him she had to run out and she'd be at her apartment—*because you didn't leave me a key,* she wrote. She jotted down her cell phone number, then signed it *Juliana* and underlined her name three times.

It took her about ten minutes to drive to her dad's house in Bay St. Louis. Turning into the driveway sent nostalgia rippling through her and caused tears to sting her eyes. Even after she'd moved into her own apartment, she'd visited him a couple of times a week.

Leaves crunched under her feet as she walked up to the porch and unlocked the door. She'd intended to get someone to clean up the yard. She made a mental note to get that done as soon as possible.

Stepping inside, she was overwhelmed by a rush of conflicting feelings. The smell of the house was familiar—she'd lived here all her life. It smelled like wood smoke and dust and the Old Spice aftershave her dad had always used.

Every time she came here, she argued with herself about what she should do about the house. It was paid for, but she couldn't decide whether to sell it or live here. Either way, she'd be set for life.

She wiped her face, trying at the same time to wipe those thoughts from her head. They were for another day. She was here for a specific reason—to find the name that was hovering just out of reach of her conscious mind.

She went directly to her bedroom, where all her yearbooks were stored on a shelf in her closet. She pulled a chair over to the closet and got down an armful of books, tossed them on her bed, then took her boots off and sat against the pillows to page through them.

An hour and a half later, she'd gone through all four years of high school and her freshman year of college. She'd found a Knoblock among the freshmen at the University of Southern Mississippi, but his photo didn't look familiar at all. During her sophomore year in high school, a girl named Sandra Kaplan had joined her class. She'd set the book aside to take with her, but from what she remembered, the girl's father was a pharmacist, not an architect.

She straightened and arched her back, groaning at the stiffness. She was thirsty and beginning to get hungry. She looked up at the closet shelf and grimaced. There were eight years of grade school that she needed to go through before she gave up. Twice as many as she'd already done.

But where to start? Might as well start at the beginning. She pulled down the yearbooks for her first four grades of school. She started with grade one.

And hit the jackpot. The last name listed in the first grade was Anthony Vega. He was a dark-haired boy with a cute grin. She frowned, studying the tiny photo. She'd have never remembered him by his picture. But looking at the printed name below the photo sent a profound relief through her and quieted the bothersome tickle at the back of her brain.

What were the chances he was related to Tito Vega? Not very good, she thought. Why would someone like Vega send his kid to public school?

That thought triggered another. How long had Anthony Vega stayed in her class? He hadn't been in any of the high school photos.

Quickly, she paged through her fourth-grade yearbook and there he was. So she climbed back onto the chair and grabbed her eighth-grade book. No Anthony Vega. So he'd left Bay High School after the fourth grade and before the eighth grade. Staying on the chair, she pulled the seventh-grade yearbook out from the stack. No Anthony Vega.

Sixth grade told a different story. His sixth-grade picture was sullen and seemed vaguely familiar. Maybe he'd been surly more often than cheerful.

In all her research, she hadn't found any information about Tito Vega's family, except for the occasional mention of his wife when they attended a party or a fundraiser. But now she had a connection between herself and Tito Vega. *If* Anthony Vega was Tito Vega's son.

She put her shoes back on, grabbed up the first-, sixth- and seventh-grade books and headed toward the front door, but then she remembered there was one more thing she needed to do.

When she'd pulled the legal papers—deeds, insurance,

will—from the safe in his den, she'd noticed a portfolio with the Golden Galaxy logo on it. But she'd forgotten about it.

She went into the den at the front of the house and turned on the lights. The safe was behind her senior portrait, which hung opposite her dad's office chair. She quickly dialed in the combination—her birthday—opened the door and pulled out the black leather portfolio, leaving the safe empty.

She looked at the clock sitting on his desk. It was after six o'clock and dark outside, and she was hungry and anxious to get back to Dawson's condo.

*No,* the little voice in her head reminded her. *We're not going to his condo. We're going back to our apartment.* It dismayed her that suddenly she didn't want to be alone. She'd always prided herself on her independence. She'd never been afraid to be out at night.

But then she'd never been attacked before.

Suppressing a shiver, she picked up the yearbooks, set the portfolio on top and started toward the front door.

She felt her phone vibrating before it rang. It was probably Dawson. Her heart fluttered as she dug into the side pocket of her purse. "Hello?" she said.

"This is just a taste of what will happen if you don't stop nosing around," a gruff voice said.

Shock burned Juliana's scalp and raised hairs on the back of her neck. "What? Who is this?"

But the phone went dead.

Juliana stared at the number on her phone's screen, trying to make sense of what the man had said.

Suddenly, all she could see was the tiny screen. She looked up. The lights had gone out. Her heart jumped into her throat and her muscles tensed. She clutched the books tightly and turned toward the study door.

She was ready to run—but where? She set the books down on the edge of the desk and pulled her gun from her purse, thumbing the safety off. Then she eased toward the door. Her throat was clogged with panic and her shoulders and neck ached from tension.

*This is just a taste,* the voice had said. *This* wasn't just a phone call and lights going out. Something was about to happen.

She put her back against the wall to the left of the door frame and listened. She couldn't hear anything.

Carefully, she rose to the balls of her feet, holding her gun in her right hand and steadying it with her left. She blinked, wishing her night vision would hurry up and kick in. She took a deep breath, then another, and angled around the door and pressed her back against the wall, her weapon leading the way. She whirled left, then right. The hallway was empty.

She stopped again to listen. Everything was quiet—too quiet. It was that odd time after rush hour when most people were home, getting dinner ready or preparing to go out for the evening. There didn't seem to be any traffic. Maybe the voice had just been trying to scare her.

*This is just a taste.* Then the rumble of a car's engine broke the silence outside. It sounded close, as if it were right in front of her house. But to see out, she'd have to go into the living room.

She held her breath, trying to listen past the engine's rumble. If someone was preparing to break into the house, or was already inside, they might use the noise of the car to mask their movements. Then the engine's noise grew fainter. They were leaving.

A crash hit her ears—breaking glass. Shock paralyzed her for an instant. She almost dropped her gun.

The crash came from the living room. Someone had broken in the big picture window. She held her breath, listening. Were they inside? Every muscle in her body shrieked with tension as she fought the urge to run.

*Don't panic. Think.*

Then light flickered red and yellow, sending writhing shadows chasing around the walls and floor and she smelled smoke.

*Fire.* Whatever they'd thrown through the window was burning. She had to get out. She glanced toward the front door. It was about fifteen feet away.

But what if that was their plan? For her to run out the front door right into their clutches.

She slid sideways along the wall toward the kitchen. She could fortify herself there. She'd be ready for anyone who came in through the front and she could guard the back door at the same time.

Halfway up the hall, she froze. She'd left her yearbooks and her dad's portfolio on the desk in the den. But she couldn't go back. It was too dangerous.

She'd have to get them later, if they survived the fire.

The fire's light and shadow beat her to the kitchen. And so had the smoke. And now she recognized the unmistakable smell of gasoline. Molotov cocktail probably. She didn't have much time. The smoke was already burning her throat.

She grabbed her phone from her purse and dialed 9-1-1. Then she called Dawson. By the time his phone rang once, she heard the faint sound of sirens. A second later, the car engine roared and tires screeched.

"Jules?" Dawson's voice in her ear sent relief gushing through her. "Damn it! Where the hell are you? I told you to—"

"I'm at my dad's. It's on fire!" she gasped out as smoke burned her throat.

"Call 9-1-1! Then get out! Stay low and get out! I'm coming!"

"I just— I am! I will." Suddenly, she felt heat buffet her like a giant's breath. "Dawson, hurry!"

She dropped her phone into her purse and ran to the back door. Her eyes were burning as much as her throat, and the air was thick with smoke.

She grabbed the knob and jerked. Then she remembered. Dead bolts. She'd installed them after her dad died to keep out burglars and vandals. She dug down into her purse with her left hand, but she couldn't find the keys. Had she left them in the front door? In her room? In the den?

The roar of the fire battled with the sirens, which were getting louder and louder. The noise was making her dizzy. She closed her eyes and leaned her shoulder against the wall by the door, still rummaging in her purse for her keys.

She took a deep breath and smoke seared her throat, triggering a coughing fit that left her completely out of breath. Gasping, she felt panic clawing its way up her throat. She heard Dawson's voice in her head.

*Get out! Stay low!*

She crouched down, breathing cautiously. The air near the floor was less thick with smoke, but she was still coughing every breath, and her eyes were pouring tears.

Feeling for the doorknob with her left hand, she pulled herself to her feet, holding her breath. Then she swung the gun's barrel at the panes of glass in the door.

Glass shattered. She swung again—once, twice, three times. Cold, sweet air hit her face. At the same time, a searing wind hit her from behind, nearly throwing her into the door.

The whole sky was ablaze with red blinking lights and the sirens screeched so loud they hurt her ears.

"Help!" she cried, her voice catching on a racking cough. "Help—me!" She fell back to the floor, her whole body spasming with the effort to breathe.

"Daw—son—"

## Chapter Twelve

Dawson cut the engine and jumped out of his car, hitting the ground running.

Black smoke and red-and-yellow flames were visible through the house's front windows. Four firefighters wrestled water hoses and two had just battered in the front door.

Dawson sprinted toward the door, but he ran into a stone wall. He blinked and realized the wall was actually a big man in a fire-retardant jacket. "Hold it!" the man shouted.

"She's in there!" Dawson yelled back, fighting to get away.

The man's strong hands gripped his shoulders. "Where?"

"I don't know! She called me!"

Using one hand to trigger his shoulder mic, the man shouted, "Check the back! We may have a female in the house! Call the EMTs."

"On it, Chief. Out."

Dawson barely heard the tinny response over the sirens and fire and the surge of pressurized water.

He wrestled with the fire chief. "Let me go!" he growled, pushing at him without effect. Then he felt the man's grip slacken.

"Not the front!" the chief shouted. "Go that way." He pointed toward the back of the house.

Dawson ran.

By the time he got around back, the door was in splinters

and a firefighter was carrying Juliana's limp form over his shoulder.

"Juliana!" he shouted, rushing forward. She didn't stir and the man carrying her paid no attention to him. He trudged on to the end of the driveway and laid her on a waiting blanket.

Dawson followed, fighting panic and a sick dread. Was she moving? Was she breathing? As soon as the fireman laid her down, he crouched beside her.

"Where's the ambulance?" he demanded as the fireman felt her pulse and listened to her breathing.

Her chest was moving, but barely. Was she getting enough air? At that instant another firefighter set a portable tank down and placed an air mask over her nose and mouth.

He watched with the other men as her chest expanded slightly, then she arched, coughing and sputtering.

Dawson reached for her arm, but the fireman shook his head. So he crouched there, helpless, as the firefighters cared for her.

A new wail pierced the air and red lights came speeding toward them. The ambulance.

Dawson took Jules's limp hand in his. This time the fireman didn't object. But within seconds, two EMTs were out of the ambulance and pushing him and the firemen out of the way. One of them replaced the fireman's air mask with one of their own, while the other listened to her breathing, looked at her eyes and felt her pulse.

Standing, he grabbed a portable gurney out of the back of the ambulance and opened it. Within seconds, they had Jules inside the ambulance and were hooking her up to machines and IVs.

Dawson started to climb in.

"Hey," the lead EMT said, holding up a hand. "Sorry, I can't allow anyone in the ambulance."

"You've got to. I've got to go with her."

"Gulfport Memorial. Meet us there."

The fire chief laid a hand on Dawson's shoulder. "You can meet them in the emergency room. She's in good hands."

Dawson wanted to protest. Actually, he wanted to hit somebody, throw something and force his way onto the ambulance, but he reined in his frustration and anger. He nodded. "Okay. Fine."

"First, son, I need to ask you a few questions."

"But—" Dawson looked at the ambulance, which was pulling away from the curb.

"I told you, she's in good hands. I don't think she's injured. I think it's just smoke inhalation," the chief said. "Come on, I need your help."

Dawson relented. He spent about a half hour giving the fire chief information about Juliana, her dad and the Sky Walk's collapse. He told him that Detective Brian Hardy was handling the case, and described the other two attempts to harm her.

Then he drove to the hospital. An E.R. nurse led him to a cubicle where Jules lay on a hospital bed. Except for her cloud of black hair, she was almost unrecognizable. She had a wet cloth over her eyes and the oxygen mask over her face. She was hooked up to an IV and a whole bunch of monitors. A machine beeped incessantly as a shiny line peaked and fell over and over on a monitor screen.

"Why does she still have that mask on?" he whispered. "Why can't she use the little—" He made a gesture with his fingers at his nose. He had no idea what the thing was called. "It's not breathing for her, is it?"

The nurse shook her head. "No, that's not a ventilator. It's just a full oxygen mask. She inhaled a lot of smoke. It delivers more oxygen," the nurse said. "When the doctor comes back and checks her out, he'll probably change it."

Dawson breathed a sigh of relief, but he was still terrified for Juliana. The part of her face he could see was so white that the yellowing bruise on her cheek stood out in ugly contrast. It hurt his heart to see her like that. "Why isn't she awake?"

"We gave her a sedative and a painkiller. She was coughing and struggling against the mask."

He nodded, not taking his eyes off her. "Can I stay with her?" he asked. "She doesn't have any family."

The nurse smiled at him. "Of course." She checked the monitor, fiddled with the IV for a couple of seconds and headed out of the cubicle.

"Nurse?" he said. "Will they keep her overnight?"

"I don't know. We'll have to wait for the doctor."

"What do you think?" Dawson persisted.

"I think she's suffering from smoke inhalation. She's fairly heavily medicated. But I'm not sure if there's a bed available. We'll see what the doctor says."

"Thanks," Dawson said as she left. He pulled the only chair in the cubicle up to the bed and sat down, but he couldn't stay still, so he kicked it back and stood. He held Jules's hand in his, running his thumb over her knuckles. He bent down to kiss it and smelled the smoke from the fire on her skin.

"Jules," he whispered. "I thought I'd lost you."

She didn't move.

JULIANA WOKE UP with her throat hurting and her eyes burning. She moaned. Did she have the flu? She coughed, but coughing didn't help. It just triggered more coughing.

She felt a warm hand slide behind her back and lift her off the pillows. A pink plastic cup with a big straw appeared in front of her face.

*Yes.* Thirsty. She reached for the cup, but her right hand felt heavy. She had to make do with her left.

"It's okay, Jules. I'll help you." The voice was low and rumbly and familiar.

"Who—" Her eyes followed the hand up to the elbow and on to the shoulder, neck and finally face. It was Dawson. She smiled. "Dawson," she whispered.

He smiled at her. "It's good to see you, too. Drink." He guided the straw into her mouth and she took a long gulp of cool water.

"Good. When you finish this cup of water the nurse said she'll take the IV out."

"IV?" Juliana looked at him, then down at her hand. It was bandaged and a clear tube ran under a bandage on the back. For an instant, panic seized her, but then the memories rushed back—all of them crowding her brain at once. She couldn't sort them out. All she could do was react.

"Oh, Dawson! Daddy's house! It's on fire!" she cried, pushing the cup away. "I've got to—"

"The fire's over," Dawson said. "Shh. It's all over now. You're in the hospital, in the emergency room—"

"Hospital?" she repeated, the panic clawing its way up her throat again. "Why? What's wrong?"

"Hey, Jules, try to stay calm. Everything's okay. It's Sunday morning. You breathed in a lot of smoke, so they wanted to keep an eye on you." He touched the tip of her nose. "You've got an oxygen tube right there."

She tried to look down at it, earning a soft chuckle from him. "But—"

"They're only going to keep you here until they're sure nothing else is wrong with you. I don't think it will be much longer."

The jumble in her mind was beginning to sort itself out. She blinked. "My eyes burn," she said, then quickly, "not bad. Not bad enough that I need to stay in the hospital."

"I know."

Dawson was acting strange, kind of like an awkward mother hen. He patted her right hand and held the straw up to her mouth. "Drink some more."

She shook her head. "Not now. I'll—" she cleared her throat and winced "—I will in a minute."

"How about some juice? Would you rather have juice? I can call the nurse."

"No," she said, shaking her head. "I'm fine." She needed to think and she was having trouble because Dawson was hovering. He hadn't taken his eyes off her since she'd woken up. Nor had he stopped touching her. His sharp features were softer than she'd ever seen them.

She closed her eyes. She could get used to this—being cared for, hovered over, worried about by Dawson.

But the smell of smoke was still in her nostrils, the sound of the flames still roared in her ears and the hazy, terrifying memories weren't falling into place like they should.

The last thing she remembered was calling Dawson. *No.* The last thing she remembered was breaking the glass in the door and breathing the cold fresh air.

"I tried to get out," she said.

Dawson's jaw clenched. "I know you did," he said. "The fireman said you broke the glass with the barrel of your gun."

She nodded as more memories buffeted her. They were still out of order, like a slideshow that had spilled. "I left my stuff. Dawson, you've got to take me back," she said. "The yearbooks, Daddy's portfolio. They're all in the den."

A thought struck her. "Did the den burn?"

"I don't think so. Jules, when the police get through with the house, we'll see what they'll let you have. One of the firemen gave me your purse, though," he said with a vague gesture behind him. "And your gun."

At that instant the sound of the living-room window shattering hit her brain. She gasped. "They threw a Molo-

tov cocktail!" she cried. "They were trying to burn Daddy's
house down. Why?"

Dawson's face went still. He looked past her, then down,
then back at her. "I don't think they were trying to burn the
house down."

"Well, then what were they trying to do? Kill me?"

Dawson's hand was still on her back. He moved it up to
her shoulder and squeezed gently, comfortingly.

"Oh, my God! They were!" Her throat started tickling
again and she coughed. That cough triggered others.

Dawson held the cup for her when she was finally able to
get her breath. She drank a few swallows.

"But why would they do that? I could have just run out the
back."

Dawson's brows drew down in a scowl. "I think they were
trying to scare you. Whoever sent them obviously doesn't
want you looking into the Sky Walk's collapse. It's probably
a good thing that your dead bolt was locked. If you'd rushed
outside, if you hadn't called 9-1-1, you might have run right
into their trap."

Juliana pushed the cup away again and lay back against
the pillows and closed her eyes. She felt drained. "I forgot
about the dead bolts," she whispered. "I was so scared."

She felt Dawson's warm firm lips on her cheek. "Why am
I so sleepy?"

"They gave you something to relax you and something for
pain."

"No kidding," she whispered. "Dawson?"

"Yeah, hon?"

She turned her hand under his and squeezed his fingers.
"Don't leave me."

IT WAS NOON BEFORE Dawson got Juliana settled in bed in his
guest room. She'd had to make a statement to Brian Hardy.

After she told Brian about the threatening phone call just seconds before the Molotov cocktail was thrown through the window, Dawson had dug her phone out of the sack of her belongings and Brian had taken down the number.

*A hundred to one it's a throwaway cell, bought with cash,* Brian had remarked. *No way in hell of tracing who bought it.*

"Shouldn't we have gone by the station to sign my statement?" Juliana asked for the third or fourth time.

"No," Dawson said patiently. "Brian said we could do that later. Are you comfortable?"

"I'm fine," she said for the twentieth or thirtieth time. "I'm not sleepy."

"I know," he said, setting a glass of water on the bedside table. "But the nurse said to put you to bed for the rest of the day, until you sleep off all that medication." He pulled the cover up a half inch, then smoothed it.

"I should take a shower," she murmured. Her eyelids were half-shut.

"Yeah, no. That's not happening. Not for a while."

"I smell like smoke," she protested, but there wasn't much resolve behind her words.

"That's true. Smoky peppermint. Very interesting."

She opened her eyes and looked at him. "I could take a bath."

"Not unless you want me to bathe you." Ah, hell, he shouldn't have said that. He'd already had to stand there in the doorway averting his eyes while she got undressed and put on pajamas—blue ones this time. Oddly, they still said Pink on the front.

Now he'd opened his big mouth and joked about bathing her, and planted that image in his head and that stirring in his groin. He huffed and shook his head, but the image wouldn't go away.

He cleared his throat. "Do you need anything?"

She shook her head with a smile. "No, Nurse Dawson." Her eyelids drifted closed. She blinked and opened them. "I guess I will nap for a little while. Don't let me sleep all day."

He nodded agreement, but she'd already drifted off.

He stood beside the bed until her breathing evened out. Then he leaned over and kissed her forehead.

"Sweet dreams, sleeping beauty," he whispered. "I promise you, I'm not going anywhere." He slipped out of the room and eased the door shut.

Then he went into the living room and lay down on the couch. He threw an arm over his face and tried to go to sleep, but images kept flashing through his mind.

Jules trapped in the burning house, screaming for him.

Jules in the bathtub, her rounded breasts glistening with water and soap, beckoning him to join her.

Jules in his arms, abandoning all restraint as he stroked her to climax.

He growled and sat up. He'd been up all night, but there was no way he was going to sleep—not anytime soon. So he took a shower in record time and made a pot of coffee.

Back on the couch, he picked up the folders that Jules had guarded with her life ever since he'd last seen them. She'd said that he could look at them. Okay, to be fair, she'd said they could go over them together, but that was practically the same thing, right?

It took him about two hours to read through every last page in every folder. Once he was done, he knew little more than he had before.

The thickest folder was all about the Delancey family. Dawson had found printouts of webpages, newspaper articles and notes about his dad, his mother, his brothers and himself. But those few pages didn't hold a candle to the printouts about Louisiana senator Con Delancey. Juliana had collected information about all of Con's shady politics, his mistresses, the bootlegging and illegal gambling that had allegedly supplemented the millions his wife had inherited, and even the controversy surrounding his death.

He had to hand it to her, she was thorough and she knew how to ferret out information. She'd covered public records, newspaper archives, the internet and two books that had been written about his infamous grandfather. Dawson hadn't seen one of them. It was by a locally renowned author and titled *Con Delancey: A Controversial Life, a Controversial Death.*

He read the inside flap. Sure enough, it sensationalized Con's politics and his personal life and promised to reveal the real truth about his death. He sighed and set the book aside.

The real truth was that Con's personal assistant had killed him. No one, not even Andre Broussard, the assistant, had disputed Con's proclivity for violent rages. The prosecutor convinced the jury that Broussard had finally had enough and snapped. He'd died in prison years ago, still proclaiming his innocence.

There wasn't nearly as much about Michael, but Juliana had his school records, including his degree in architectural design. She had a copy of his contractor's license, as well as newspaper articles about his indictment, his sentence and his release from prison after thirty months.

Dawson took a deep breath and shook his head. It was a lot of damning evidence—circumstantial but still damning. Juliana had done what Dawson himself had done—painted Michael Delancey with the same brush as his infamous father. And when she found out who he was, she'd do the same with him.

Dawson leafed back through the pages until he came to the newspaper article that mentioned Michael Delancey's children. He read it again, clenching his jaw as he looked at the names. *Three sons, John, Ryker and Reilly, and a daughter, Rosemary, deceased.*

*John*. No mention of his middle name. But then, there was no reason the press would know that he went by Dawson. It was his dad and granddad who were locally notorious, not him.

He set the folders back on the coffee table and stared at them. He'd been right about Jules. She'd held on to those folders so vehemently, not because there was valuable information in them, but because they were all she had left now that her dad had been killed. He was no psychologist, but it didn't take one to see that.

He understood. Once he'd decided that his dad was a crook who cared less for people's safety than he did about saving a buck, he'd clung to his independence with every bit as much determination as Jules clung to her research.

But damn it, he wished she wasn't so stubborn. He'd told her not to leave his condo. If she'd paid attention to him, her dad's house wouldn't have been firebombed. She wouldn't have come way too close to death.

How was he going to keep her safe if she wouldn't listen to him?

# Chapter Thirteen

Dawson cleared his brain of useless questions—like how to cure Juliana's stubbornness. Checking his watch, he saw that it was after two o'clock.

He'd questioned Hardy about any evidence found on the Molotov cocktail bottle, but Hardy had told him irritably that he'd have to wait until Monday. *Just like me,* he'd said.

Dawson speed-dialed his brother Ryker. No answer. He tried Reilly.

"What's up, Daw?" Reilly said affably.

"Hey, Reilly, where's your brother?"

"I think he and Nicole went to the aquarium. He said he was off duty, so he was turning his cell phone off. What's going on?"

"I need to check out a fire in Bay St. Louis last night. It was started by a Molotov cocktail."

"Something to do with a client?"

"Yeah, you could say that."

"I'm off duty today, too. I could go in and see what I can find if you really need me to, but Christy and I were about to head over to Mom and Dad's. We're going to take them out to dinner this evening."

"No, you guys go on and have fun. Let me know what you think about Mom."

"I can tell you right now. She's doing good. *I* see them about once a week. So does Ryker."

Dawson started to fire back a cutting retort, but he wasn't in the mood. "Say hi for me," he said. "Talk to you later."

As he hung up, he heard the guest-room door open and the bathroom door close. He started to jump up and check on Juliana to see if she needed anything, but he decided to wait. Was she just up for a moment to go to the bathroom? Or was she taking a shower?

He heard the water turn on. She'd slept a couple more hours after sleeping nearly all night in the E.R., so maybe she wasn't too drowsy to take a shower. He stood and paced, straining his ears, hoping he wouldn't miss hearing her if she fell.

Finally he heard the water turn off and about ten minutes later, she appeared in the living-room doorway. She'd dried her hair and it floated around her shoulders, framing her face, which was still pale. She'd put on a long-sleeved pullover shirt and gray pants and had on pink fuzzy slippers.

Dawson's mouth went dry at the sight of her. It didn't matter that she was fully dressed. He had to clamp his jaw to stop the instant replay of the erotic vision of her all wet and glistening.

"Did you get your nap out?" he asked, wincing when he heard the gruffness in his voice.

A small wrinkle appeared between her brows. "Yes. At least I think so." She yawned. "The hot shower made me feel drowsy again."

*And it made me feel horny,* Dawson thought. "You want to go back to bed?" he asked.

"Actually, I'm hungry," she said, crossing her arms and walking over to perch on the edge of the couch. "Got anything to eat?"

He shrugged. "I don't know. I don't cook much, but I might have some cheese. I make a mean grilled cheese sandwich."

"That sounds great. I don't even remember when I ate last."

"Me either," he replied. "It takes about ten minutes to make a really great grilled cheese. Get some coffee while I fix them."

Juliana followed him into the kitchen and poured herself a cup of coffee. "Wow!" she exclaimed after taking a sip.

"Too strong?" he asked.

"A little bit," she responded. "Got any cream or milk?"

He shook his head as he dug a skillet out and set it on the stove. "Just canned. In the refrigerator."

She poured some into her coffee and took her mug to the kitchen table and sat.

"How's your throat?" he asked as he put the sandwiches together and put them into the skillet where butter was sizzling.

"Okay," she said, sipping the coffee. "It just feels a little raw. When we finish eating, can we go over to my dad's house? I want to see it, and I need to get those books."

"I told you last night, the police will let us know when you can get in there." Dawson slid the grilled cheese sandwich onto a plate and cut it in half.

"There you go," he said as he set the plate in front of her with a little flourish.

"How long do you think it will be? I need those books."

"Maybe tomorrow." He put the second sandwich in the pan and adjusted the heat.

"Can we just drive by? I want to see how badly the house was burned," she said, then took a bite of sandwich. "This is *good*."

"Told you." Dawson grinned as he served up his own sandwich and sat down across the table from her.

She devoured the sandwich in record time and drained her coffee mug. Dawson finished just a few seconds after her. She stood and took their plates to the sink. "I'll do the dishes."

"No, you won't," he said, standing behind her. "Get out of the way. I'll wash them. You need to go lie down."

She turned on the hot water and squirted dishwashing liquid into the pan.

"Come on," he said, moving next to her and bumping her with his hip. "You'd better take advantage of me while I'm in a good mood."

She turned and plopped a handful of suds on his nose. The handful was too big for just his nose, though, so it got in his mouth. He sputtered, laughing. "What are you doing? You'd better watch out."

She laughed at him and blew on the suds. He felt her breath tickle his lips, and before he even thought about what he was doing, he leaned down and rubbed the soap suds from his face onto hers. Then he kissed her.

She squealed and cried, "Eww," but he didn't stop. He urged her mouth open and thrust his tongue inside, kissing her deeply. Not even the taste of soap killed his desire. He felt her tongue on his, and a spear of lust hit him squarely in the groin. He hardened immediately.

His hands cupped her backside. He pulled her against him. She gasped and rose on her tiptoes, pressing herself closer and returning his kiss with matching passion.

"Damn it, Jules," he whispered hoarsely. "You're killing me."

In answer, she ran her hand down his chest to his belly and farther, finally gripping the button on his jeans. She fumbled with it as she bit his earlobe and teased it with her tongue.

Pushing her hand away, he opened his fly. She slid her thumbs inside his jeans and pushed them down a few inches, then she took him in her hand.

He nearly cried out as his erection pulsed against her palm. "You've got to stop," he begged her, but the only answer he got was a low, throaty chuckle.

So he jerked her sweatpants down, and in one smooth motion, he lifted her and set her down on the kitchen table. Then he touched her, urging her legs apart.

She moaned and thrust toward his hand. "Dawson," she gasped. "Please—"

It was all the invitation he needed. He pulled her to the edge of the table and entered her, smoothly and slowly. She was ready for him. She met him thrust for thrust. She lifted her face to his and kissed him hard and long, the rhythm of their kisses in sync with the rhythm of their lovemaking.

Dawson felt her body change and open. She threw her head back and cried out as he allowed his own climax to overtake him. They came together.

Afterward, Dawson held her in his arms with her head resting against his shoulder. Her hot breath whispered over his skin. When he finally pulled away, Jules looked at him with heavy-lidded eyes.

"Want to take a nap?" she whispered.

He closed his eyes and rubbed his nose against hers. "No," he said softly. "But I would like to go to bed."

JULIANA WOKE WITH A START. *Fire. Dawson.* But she wasn't in her dad's house, breathing smoke. She was with Dawson in his bed. He was beside her, asleep.

Then the real memories came back to her. Memories of Dawson making love to her on his kitchen table, proving to her that their first time hadn't been a fluke. They'd gone to his bedroom and he'd proven it to her again.

She was a believer now. She turned her head and looked across the little mound of white sheets at him. His intense blue eyes were closed and his mouth was relaxed. He looked like he didn't have a care in the world. She propped herself on her elbow and leaned down to kiss his cheek.

He muttered something that she couldn't understand, but he didn't wake up. It occurred to her that while she'd been sedated all night in the emergency room, he'd been awake. He probably had not slept a wink. He'd been watching her.

Watching over her.

Tears filled her eyes. Oh, how wonderful it would be if she could have him to watch over her for the rest of her life. Well, and keep taking her to those incredible heights of pleasure.

She slipped out of bed and pulled on her sweatpants and top. He might be exhausted, but she'd gotten all the sleep she needed. More than enough. She was feeling antsy.

When she stepped into the living room, it was dark outside. If she added it all up, she'd probably slept close to twenty-four hours.

The kitchen clock read after six. And she was hungry. Dawson's grilled cheese sandwich had been good, but it was long gone by now.

She went into the kitchen to look around for something to eat. In the refrigerator was more cheese, the canned milk, half a loaf of bread and some butter. The freezer yielded up little more. There was a pint of ice cream that was over half-empty. A bag of frozen French fries had definitely seen better days.

In the pantry, she found a couple of cans of chili, a big can of peanuts and a bottle of pancake syrup. She shuddered to think about how all that would taste in one dish.

She was considering chili and cheese when she heard Dawson's cell phone ringing. She went looking for it, wondering if she should wake him. It was on the couch where he'd been sitting. She picked it up and looked at the display—and froze.

The name on the display said Michael Delancey. For a couple of seconds, Juliana stared at it, numb with shock. She couldn't move, couldn't breathe. She blinked hard and looked at the display again, but nothing changed.

Why would Michael Delancey call Dawson?

She couldn't think of a reason. Not a good one anyway. Was Michael Delancey his client?

No. She shook her head. Dawson wouldn't do that to her, would he? With a thumb that was shaking so badly she could barely control it, she answered it.

Sirens and car horns screamed through the phone. Before she could draw breath to say hello, a panicked male voice was shouting.

"Dawson, the house is on fire! Your mother and I are all right. Dear God, it's a mess. Dawson?"

Juliana opened her mouth, but nothing came out.

"Dawson! Are you there?"

"Jules?"

She looked at him. He stood in the doorway, his hair tousled and his eyes heavy-lidded with sleep. But as soon as he saw the phone in her hand, he stalked over and took it from her, his fingers touching hers. She jerked them away.

His jaw tensed as he glanced at the display, then held the phone to his ear. "Dad?"

The single syllable stabbed Juliana in the heart. She heard Michael Delancey's voice, and behind it the wail of sirens. "Son, did you hear me?"

"No! Tell me." His eyes were on her, burning like lasers in his dangerously scowling face.

"The house is on fire!"

"Are you okay? Mom?"

"We're fine. I just—"

"Dad, I'll be right there. Don't worry." He hung up and stuck the phone in his jeans pocket. Without a word he whirled and headed to his room.

Juliana couldn't think. Her brain was stuttering like a

scratched CD. Michael Delancey. *Michael—Michael. De—De—De—Delancey.* She pressed her palms against her eyes and shook her head.

*Think!*

But all her brain would do was replay those words that had cut her heart like a knife. *Son. Dad.*

Dawson came out of his room, talking on the phone. "I'm on my way. Have you talked to Reilly?"

Juliana watched him. It was like watching a car wreck. She couldn't tear her eyes away. He'd thrown on a sweatshirt and run his fingers through his hair.

"Do you know how it started? No? Okay, I'll see you there." He hung up and stuck the phone in his jeans, then looked at her.

"I've got to go," he said. His eyes weren't lasers now. He looked worried and—if she could read him—embarrassed. But she couldn't read him.

Why had she ever thought she'd seen sincerity and honor in this man who had lied to her from the first moment she'd laid eyes on him? She finally managed to tear her gaze away. She nodded once, stiffly.

He headed to the kitchen, then turned back. "Jules, if you're thinking about leaving, don't. This has to be the same people who firebombed your dad's house. It's too dangerous out there."

She lifted her chin.

"Promise me you'll stay here."

"You lied to me. I don't ever want to talk to you again."

"I'll lock you in if you don't promise me."

"I'll stay here," she said, her voice flat. "Just leave."

He studied her for a few seconds, then clenched his jaw, turned and left. She heard the kitchen door slam, heard his car start, heard the garage door open, then shut.

For another minute or so, she just stood there, the image of the phone's display still stuck in her brain.

*Michael Delancey.*

Then she went into the guest room and started packing. She said the words he'd demanded. *I'll stay here.* But she'd seen in his eyes that he knew she was lying. She had to get out of here.

But his words had frightened her. *The same people. It's too dangerous out there.* She thought of everything that had happened, the attack at the post office, the falling beam, the fire at her dad's house. Was he right?

She shivered. Damn him. This was his fault. She'd come to depend on his being there to protect her.

Why hadn't she listened to her little voice? He had never intended to protect her. Everything he'd done had been to protect his father, Michael Delancey, the man who'd caused her dad's death.

## *Chapter Fourteen*

Dawson sped over to his parents' house in his Corvette, trying to focus on getting there and making sure his parents were all right. But his brain was spinning faster than the wheels of the Vette.

The fire had to be the work of the same people who'd torched Vincent Caprese's house, just like he'd told Jules. He'd tell Ryker, get him to find out what evidence the police had found on the bottle. Had this fire been the result of a Molotov cocktail? Thank God his mom and dad had gotten out without being hurt. Now if Jules would just listen to him and stay put. But he knew she wouldn't. He should have locked her in.

All that swirled in his brain in the thirty minutes it took to get to his parents' house in Chef Voleur.

He spotted the black smoke while he was still several blocks away from his parents' street. As he whipped the Vette around the corner of their street his brain registered two fire trucks. He roared up to the curb, killed the engine and jumped out. As he did, a couple of firemen who were busy wrapping up the water hoses glanced his way.

He spotted his mom right away and ran toward her. "Mom!" he called.

"J.D.," she cried and held out her arms.

He grabbed her and hugged her. She smelled like smoke. "Are you okay? You're not hurt, are you?"

She shook her head. "Look at my house," she said. "Who would do this?"

The flames were out, but smoke still drifted upward from the front door and the broken window. "Where's Dad?"

She pointed. "Over there talking to the fire chief."

The man his dad was talking to was the same man who'd been at Caprese's house the night before. He squeezed his mother's shoulder. "Are you sure you're okay?"

She gave him a wan smile. "I'm fine. You go talk to them. Find out who did this."

At that moment a car roared up and screeched to a halt behind Dawson's. He knew without looking that it was Ryker's BMW. His brother sprinted across the lawn toward them.

Dawson met Ryker's gaze and nodded as his mom turned to her second son and hugged him. Then he headed over to where his dad and the fire chief were standing.

"Dawson," his dad said in greeting. "This is Chief Jeffreys. Chief, my son Dawson."

"Chief," Dawson said, offering his hand. The fire chief took it.

"We've met," the chief said to Michael. "Last night, in fact." He shook his head at Dawson. "How is it you're involved with all this?"

"I'm investigating the collapse of the Sky Walk at the Golden Galaxy Casino," Dawson said. "Apparently, there's somebody out there who doesn't like my nosing around."

The chief nodded. "This is your parents' house? And last night? Your girlfriend?"

Dawson gave a short, unamused laugh. "No, hardly my girlfriend. Vincent Caprese was her dad. He was killed when the Sky Walk collapsed. She's been nosing around, too."

"Maybe you two should stop *nosing* before somebody gets killed."

"There was a fire last night? Involving Vincent Caprese's daughter?" His dad frowned at him. "Why didn't you tell me?"

Dawson sighed. "I've been a little busy, Dad."

The chief glanced at each of them in turn. "I tell you what. The police are on their way. They're going to want to talk to you both about all this. I've got to get my men rounded up and make my report."

Michael held out his hand. "Thanks, Chief. I appreciate it. You and your men did a great job."

Dawson held out his own hand in turn. "That's right. Thanks."

The chief eyed Dawson. "I don't want to see you at another fire," he said.

"Trust me, I'm not planning to be at another one," Dawson replied.

Once the chief walked over to the fire truck, Michael turned to Dawson. "What was going on with your phone? Couldn't you hear me?"

Dawson grimaced. "Not at first," he hedged. "I'm here, though. What happened exactly?"

Ryker walked up, followed by Reilly and their mom. The twins had matching scowls on their faces. After quick hugs and greetings all around, Dawson repeated his question.

Michael wiped a hand down his face. "I was downstairs. Your mother was finishing up the dishes. I heard glass breaking." He reached for his wife's hand. "I thought she'd dropped something, so I started upstairs to check. Then she screamed."

"I heard the big window in the front shatter." She pointed to the hole in the floor-to-ceiling window in the two-story-high foyer. "I ran in there to see what had happened and flames were coming out of a broken bottle."

"A Molotov cocktail," Reilly said.

Dawson nodded.

"I screamed for your father and ran to get some water, but by the time he got up from the basement, the sheer curtains on the side windows were up in flames. We ran out through the garage."

"I called 9-1-1 after we were outside," Michael put in.

Ryker turned to Dawson. "This is all connected to the Sky Walk, isn't it? Who are these people? Do you know?"

Dawson shook his head. "No, but I'm sure as hell going to find out. In fact, I need you to—" He was cut off by the sound of police sirens. Two police vehicles roared up and two officers got out of one, while two young men in casual attire jumped out of the second, carrying cases.

"There's the crime scene unit," Reilly said. "I'm going to go talk to them, see if I can observe."

Ryker started to follow him, but Dawson caught his arm. "I need the evidence from the bottle, plus their findings from Caprese's house last night. This is getting way too close to home."

"You got that right. Why don't you back off and let the police handle this? Your snooping around is just muddying the water, not to mention putting our parents' lives in danger."

Dawson glanced toward the house. "I think I'm getting close to the truth. Why would they target Mom and Dad?"

Ryker took a step toward him. "Maybe they think you're smarter than you are."

"What the hell's that supposed to mean?"

"I'm guessing this is a message to you to back off."

"I'm not backing off. There have already been three attempts to hurt or kill Jules and the police refuse to put her in protective custody."

"Oh, come on, Daw. I know you—you're a maverick. You'd rather work against the police than with them."

"So? I'm getting results."

"Results? You think two deliberate fire assaults are results?"

Dawson scowled at his younger brother. "If I don't figure out what's going on, Dad could go back to jail."

"He can't go back to jail if he's dead," Ryker shot back.

"Look at that," Dawson shouted, gesturing toward the house. "Do you think for one minute that they couldn't have broken in and killed Mom and Dad? The Molotov cocktail was a warning."

"That's what I said! A warning to *you*. Too bad you don't have sense enough to take it!"

"Dawson! Ryker!"

Dawson turned and stared. Michael Delancey's voice sounded stronger and sharper than it had in years.

Ryker took a step backward. "I'm going to talk to the officers," he said shortly and walked away.

"Is Ryker right?" Michael asked Dawson.

"About what?" Dawson growled.

"Are you the one these people are trying to stop?"

"It's Jules—Juliana Caprese—who's being targeted."

His dad studied him for a few seconds. "Until tonight. Now it's your mother and me."

Dawson didn't say anything.

"You listen to me, son. If you're fooling around in Tito Vega's business, you'd better stop. He ruined my life without lifting a finger. If he was behind the Sky Walk's collapse, he won't let you live long enough to expose him."

DAWSON WAITED UNTIL EVERYONE had gone and his mom was packing a bag to go to a hotel to corner his dad.

"I want the truth, Dad. Now!" Dawson growled. They were

standing on the brick entrance to the house, looking at the damage.

"That stained-glass insert is a Tiffany," Michael said. "Your grandmother gave it to us."

Dawson looked up at the colorful circle, the bottom few panes of which were broken. He'd never paid any attention to it. It was just a part of the house he'd grown up in. "Maybe you can get it fixed," he said distractedly, then, "Dad—"

"Don't start with me. This has been a horrible night. I don't want Edie to come out and hear us arguing again. She can't handle all this stress right now."

Dawson clenched his fists as he thought of his mother struggling to stay sober. "Then why didn't you think about her when you were getting yourself thrown in prison?"

A pained expression crossed Michael's face. "What's it going to take to make you believe I didn't deserve to go to jail? I've never done a dishonest day's work in my life."

"You want to know what it's going to take to make me believe you? How about the whole truth? How about telling me everything you know about the Sky Walk, who worked on it, who was responsible for it falling if it's not you." Dawson blew out a frustrated breath. "Tell me now, before someone else gets hurt."

To his surprise, his dad nodded. "Okay." He sighed. "I did hire Knoblock after the guy in the suit threatened your mother. I knew he'd been sent by Vega, although he never said. So, yes, even though I knew exactly why Vega wanted Knoblock on the project, I hired him and let him handle the Sky Walk." Michael shook his head and sat down on one of the brick steps.

"He was a nervous wreck the whole time. Always looking over his shoulder, snapping at the workers. One day I was there after hours, around eight o'clock, just taking a look at everything, and I heard him on his phone. He obviously didn't think anyone was around. He was angry." Michael leaned his forearms on his knees.

"Best I can remember, his exact words were 'revenge for your son is between you and him. I've taken care of everything you asked for. We're square now. My men and I will be out of here by tomorrow.'" Michael paused for a second. "Whoever was on the other end of the phone said something. Then Knoblock said, 'Fine. You keep your blood money. It'll be worth it to me if I never hear from you again.'"

Dawson frowned. "*Revenge for your son.* Who was he talking to?"

Michael shook his head. "I have no idea."

"Have you told this to the police?"

"No! And I'm not going to. If that was Vega on the phone and it gets out that I heard the conversation, he'll make good on his promise. He'll kill your mother."

"Are you sure it was Vega?" Dawson asked.

"No, I'm not sure of anything. But Vega wanted Knoblock to build the Sky Walk."

"Where's Knoblock now? I'll get him pulled in for questioning and get a warrant for his phone records."

"No idea. He came in the next day, reported to me that the job was finished, and I never saw him again. He didn't even wait for me to pay him."

"Damn it, Dad! If I'd known this, I could have had the police looking for him all this time. I saw where he'd been indicted for a bridge collapse in Kansas City. Maybe he went back there. I'll get the police to check on that."

"Don't do that, Dawson. If you do, Vega will hear. He'll know. You'll get your mother killed."

"How do you think he's going to find out?"

Michael stood and paced. "Are you kidding me? Look at the man. He's right up there with all the big-city officials and politicians. How do you think he's managed never to get caught in all this time?"

Dawson spread his hands. "I'll tell you how. Because people like you are too chicken to come forward." He stepped up to his dad. "Well, that ends right here, right now. You—" he poked a finger at his dad's chest "—are going to the police and telling them everything."

Michael lifted his chin and stared Dawson down. "I will not. I can't risk your mother's life!"

"We can get both of you into protective custody. Hell, *I'll* get a couple of my men to guard you." He turned and paced, taking the same path Michael had. "I just wish we had some proof."

He pushed his fingers through his hair. *Proof.* The police weren't going to be very impressed with a couple of notes, especially considering that Michael Delancey wrote one of them. He turned back to his dad. "Are you sure there's not—"

Michael was staring at the ground, an odd look on his face.

"There's something else, isn't there?"

The older man kept staring at the ground for several more seconds. Then he looked up at Dawson.

"Dad?"

"Can you promise me you can protect your mother? She's so—fragile right now. Her nerves are nearly shot from trying to quit drinking."

Dawson stared at his dad. "What are you saying? I can keep both of you safe, but— What are you thinking?"

"I've got proof—proof at least that the design for the Sky Walk was altered. It implicates Knoblock. It's not going to give you Vega."

Dawson's pulse raced. "You've got proof? Why didn't you tell me? Where is it? *What* is it? Is it here, in the house?"

Michael nodded. "In my safe." They went into the house and met Edie coming from the bedroom with her suitcase.

"Here, Mom, let me get that," Dawson said.

"Ready to go?" Michael asked Edie. "I'll get the papers while you put the suitcase in the car," he told Dawson, tossing him his keys.

By the time Dawson got the suitcase into the trunk of their Lexus and his mother settled in the passenger seat, Michael was there with a large envelope. He gave it to Dawson.

"That's the altered plans. You'll see Knoblock's notes about the changes." Michael shook his head. "The only thing it proves is that he compromised the structural integrity of the Sky Walk. Not who ordered it."

"Where did you get these?"

"They were in a locker in a dressing room the construction workers used. I knew Knoblock had stored some things there, but I figured he'd cleaned out his locker before he left. It was a long shot."

Dawson peered inside the envelope. The sheets of paper he saw were stained and wrinkled. "What happened to them?"

"The lockers were under the Sky Walk. Everything in them spilled out onto the floor."

"You went in there and found these *after* the collapse?"

Michael nodded. "I was hoping I could find something that proved that Knoblock was responsible." He shrugged. "That does, but it doesn't prove I'm innocent."

"What do you want me to do with them?"

"I'd bet money that Knoblock's dead. Vega wouldn't leave a loose end like that hanging. Especially not after what I overheard. But on the off chance he's managed to stay alive, maybe you can find him."

Dawson was afraid his dad was right. If Vega was behind all this, and he was on the other end of Knoblock's phone call, he might very well be dead. "I'll see what I can find."

He walked over and leaned down to speak to his mother

through the passenger window. "Mom, get some rest, and don't worry about the house, okay?"

She shook her head with a wry smile. "I'm not worried about the house, dear. I'm worried about my men." She patted his hand. "Please be careful. And don't forget what I told you about your father."

"I won't," he replied. "I'll call you tomorrow." He straightened as his dad opened the driver's-side door. "I'll call you, too, Dad."

Michael got in the car and pulled away.

Dawson watched the taillights until they disappeared around a corner, then he turned and looked at the house. Ryker was right. He'd put his parents in danger, and for what? He looked at the envelope in his hand. It might be the only solid piece of evidence he had that Knoblock changed the plans for the Sky Walk. But was it enough to clear his dad?

Sighing, he pulled out his phone and called Grey Reed, his best investigator after Mack. "Grey, you're not on assignment right now, are you?"

"Nope. I turned in the final report on the Barber case Friday."

"I need you to bodyguard my parents." He gave Grey a synopsis of what had happened and told him where they were staying. As he got into his car, he called his dad to tell him what he'd arranged. Then finally, he headed back to his apartment.

*His apartment. Jules.* Yeah, no chance she'd still be there, not now that she knew he was Michael Delancey's son.

## Chapter Fifteen

Juliana breathed a sigh of relief as she shifted the plastic bag of books to her left hand to unlock the door to her apartment. She'd made it. It was after ten o'clock, but she was finally home.

She dropped the books and her purse onto the couch and trudged into the bedroom. Without doing anything except kick off her boots, she fell onto the bed and pulled the throw over her.

She closed her eyes and waited to fall asleep. It couldn't take more than a few seconds—she was that tired. But now that she'd made it safely back here, sleep evaded her.

She turned over and pulled the throw over her head. She took a deep breath that ended at the top with a yawn, then let it out, coaxing her limbs to settle onto the mattress as her lungs deflated.

*There. Relax and go to sleep.*

But no. Her brain was on fast-forward. Everything that had happened in the past thirty-six hours or so was flashing before her closed lids like a slide show out of control.

The fire, the hospital, Dawson taking such gentle care of her, then making love to her over and over again.

And then—that phone call.

She threw off the throw and sat up. She couldn't sleep. Tossing her clothes on the floor of her closet, she headed into the bathroom and took a hot shower. It made her feel better but it didn't stop the images from spinning in her head.

As she towel dried her hair, the image of Dawson as he'd looked standing in the living-room doorway rose in her mind. He'd looked horrified, chagrined, embarrassed. As well he should have.

But no matter how horrified he was that she was holding his cell phone, staring at the display, his horror hadn't held a candle to hers.

Dawson was Michael Delancey's son.

How could she have been so naive, so stupid? She'd been suspicious of him from the first moment he'd stepped in front of her to pay the taxi driver. She should have checked him out further. Somewhere on the internet was a mention of his full name, she was sure. He was John Dawson Delancey.

She tossed the towel onto the floor and threw on her terry cloth robe, then headed into the kitchen to see what she had in her freezer. She knew that whatever was in the refrigerator was probably growing green mold by now.

Ice cream. Perfect. She'd give herself brain freeze. That would stop the slide show. But did she have any chocolate syrup? She opened the refrigerator door, ignoring the green stuff, and found it. Squeezing an ignominious amount onto her two scoops of ice cream, she went into the living room and plopped down on the couch.

She took a big bite of vanilla ice cream swimming in chocolate syrup and closed her eyes as the dark sweetness and icy cold stung the roof of her mouth. She took another bite. It was necessary to eat fast to get brain freeze. Then she reached for the remote control—silly sitcoms went well with brain freeze—but instead she found herself reaching into the bag of books she'd retrieved from her dad's den.

As soon as Dawson left to check on his parents—the Delanceys—she'd called a cab to take her to her dad's. The house might be a crime scene, but she still had keys, so she'd gone inside. She'd studiously ignored the damage and headed directly to the den and grabbed the yearbooks and portfolio she'd left there.

She had no idea what was in the portfolio. When she'd glanced inside, all she'd seen were small, black bound notebooks, like day planners.

She emptied them onto the couch beside her. Picking up the notebooks one by one, she saw that they actually were day planners—eleven of them, one for each of the past eleven years, except for this current year. She flipped through a couple of them. Her dad had kept a record of his life, measured out in pages divided into hours and half hours. And in the back of the recent ones were a pile of sticky notes.

Her throat closed and her eyes grew damp, looking at the pages of her father's life. She had vague recollections of his reaching into his shirt pocket for a black book and jotting notes into it, but it had never occurred to her that one day he would be gone and she would be reading the events of his life in his own handwriting, hoping to find a clue to why he'd died.

But where was this year's planner? Then she remembered—she'd found it in his desk at the casino. Dawson had put it in her purse, along with the other things she'd found there.

She grabbed her purse and dug inside until she found the day planner. She stared at its cover for a long while.

She didn't think she wanted to read the entries for the last day of his life. She wasn't sure she wanted to read any of them. But she'd never forgive herself if the answer to why he'd died was on one of those pages and she didn't even try to find it.

She finished the ice cream while she paged through, starting at January 1. Her dad had been semiretired before he got the job at the Golden Galaxy Casino, so the pages were filled with notes about fly-tying or woodworking projects, dates for coffee or golf with friends, and notes about her. Several times she had to stop and dry her eyes as she read things he'd written about her.

Then, on April 20, next to the 2:00 p.m. line, a name jumped out at her as if it were printed in flashing red ink.

*Vega,* written in her dad's neat, precise hand. Her heart thudded against her chest so hard that she put her hand over it.

*Vega came through. Surprise! Got call from Meadow Gold Corp. Golden Galaxy, here I come! Opening June 1. Short notice...*

It was the connection she'd been looking for. *Vega came through.* There was only one way to interpret that. He'd gotten her dad the job as manager at the Golden Galaxy. The mention of Meadow Gold Corporation implied that Vega was connected with the business.

She looked at the next page and the next. There were a number of meetings scheduled with the corporation, with the Gaming Commission, with other employees who had already been hired, but nothing else about Tito Vega.

She picked up the other notebooks and shuffled through them looking for last year's. Her dad had said *Vega came through.* That meant he'd talked to him previously, didn't it? But when?

She knew it wasn't after January 1, so she started at December 31 of the previous year and worked backward.

Then on the page for August 23, she found Vega's name.

*Tito Vega*—underlined three times—*called. re: me as Mgr Golden Galaxy Casino? Waveland. What's his angle? Prob. 6 mo.- 1 yr. Not holding breath.*

Tito Vega had gotten her dad the job at the Golden Galaxy,

but why? And what, if anything, did this have to do with her father's death?

Juliana laid the two day planners on the coffee table, open to the notes about Vega. Then she opened the yearbooks to her class's pictures. She stared at her dad's notes, then at the tiny photo of Anthony Vega in her sixth-grade yearbook.

What did it mean that she went to school with Anthony Vega? If anything. She didn't even know if Anthony was kin to Tito Vega. She picked up her folder with information she'd gathered about Vega and paged through it. There were mentions of his wife and children, but not many. His prominence along the Gulf Coast had developed over the last twenty years or so.

Anthony Vega was in her sixth-grade class but not seventh. She was eleven in the sixth grade, eighteen years ago. Maybe Tito Vega had sent his son to public school until his growing wealth made him able to afford private schools.

But even if that were true, what did it mean? Anything at all? Or was it just coincidence?

She stared at the pages, frowning, concentrating, but no flashes of inspiration came to her.

She wiped her face, then plunged her fingers into her hair. This was so frustrating. She had something here—she knew it! But she couldn't figure out what she had or what she should do with it. There was a piece of the puzzle missing. Trouble was, not only didn't she know which piece it was, but she also didn't even know where in the puzzle it fit.

She needed help. She was out of her league.

Damn it. She needed Dawson.

JULIANA WOKE UP with a cramp in her leg. Sitting up, she realized she'd fallen asleep on the couch, wrapped in her terry cloth robe. The pages were still spread out on the coffee table, next to her empty chocolate-smeared ice-cream bowl.

She pushed her hair out of her eyes. It had air dried into tangled waves. As she finger combed it, she studied the array of information she'd gathered about Tito Vega. It made no more sense this morning than it had last night.

She blew out an exasperated breath. What she'd realized last night hadn't changed. She needed Dawson's help to solve the mystery of how and why Tito Vega was involved in the collapse of the Sky Walk.

She looked at her watch. It was seven-thirty. Too early to call him? He'd probably been up late, talking to the authorities about the fire at his parents' house.

Tough. She needed her research, which she'd left at his apartment, and she needed to talk to him.

A flutter of apprehension whispered in her chest. She didn't want to talk to him. He'd lied to her—taken advantage of her. *Hurt her.*

She reached for her cell phone. Her hand hovered over it. What was she going to say? She needed to sound detached, businesslike. She couldn't let him know how much he'd hurt her.

She clasped her fingers together. Okay, here goes.

*Dawson, I need to see you. I have information that links my father with Tito Vega.* Yes, that would work.

She cleared her throat. "Dawson, I need to—" Her hand went to her neck. She sounded like a strangled frog. She got up and went to the kitchen for a glass of water. Her throat felt like the frog had taken up residence there. Taking a sip, she swallowed carefully, then tried again.

"Dawson, I need to see you." That was better.

Back in the living room, she picked up the phone and dialed Dawson's number. Taking a deep breath, she blew it out slowly as she listened to the ring.

"Yeah?" Dawson's voice sounded sleepy, gruff, sexy.

"Dawson, I need—" And then suddenly the frog was back. She swallowed with difficulty.

"Jules? Where are you? Are you all right?"

"I'm fine," she said quickly and cleared her throat, but before she could say anything, he lit into her.

"You told me you'd stay put."

Her temper flared. "You told me that we were on the same side."

"We are! We both want the truth."

"You don't want the truth! You want to keep your *dad* out of prison."

He was quiet again. "What do you want, Jules?"

She bit her tongue. No matter whose side he was on, he was the only person she could trust to help her put the puzzle pieces together.

"I need to talk to you. I've—I've found proof that Vega hired my dad to work at the Golden Galaxy Casino."

"Vega hired— I don't understand."

"I know. Me, either. Somehow all this is connected, but I can't put it together on my own. And I need my folders."

He was silent for a beat. "Is that what this is about? You want your little folders back?" he asked. "Well, I'm guessing you must have picked up your car last night, so why don't you just drive on over here and get them. I'm going to be gone anyway."

Juliana scraped her teeth across her lower lip. He sounded so harsh. If she didn't know better, she might think he sounded hurt. But she did know better. She blew out a frustrated breath.

"I wonder if you could make some time for me. I'd appreciate it."

She heard his sigh through the phone. "Fine, but I'm busy this morning. I've got to go with Mom and Dad to sign their statements about the fire and see if the police found any evidence on the bottle or in the driveway."

Juliana's heart sank. She'd expected him to sound defensive, even chagrined. But he sounded angry. *She* was the one who had a right to be angry, not him. How dare he make her feel defensive?

But she was also the one who needed him. So she'd take what she could get. "All right. This afternoon, then? Two o'clock?"

There was a brief silence on the other end of the phone. "I'll call you. I'm not sure when I'll be done."

Later than two o'clock? She couldn't sit here that long without losing her mind. She took a deep breath, prepared to yell at him that this was the first piece of real evidence they had. That it had to be Vega who was behind the Molotov cocktails. But she bit her tongue, stopping the retort. If she antagonized him, he might not agree to see her at all. After all, she'd practically thrown him out of his own apartment.

"Okay," she said, trying to mask her disappointment. "Please call me as soon as you can. This is important."

"Yeah," Dawson said, but she could tell he'd already stopped listening to her.

"Bye," she said, but he'd already broken the connection.

She set the phone on the coffee table and stared at it. It wasn't quite eight o'clock in the morning and Dawson had just ruined her entire day. She was going to have to sit here until after two o'clock, when he decided he had time to talk to her.

She looked at the sheets of paper spread out on her coffee table and shook her head. She couldn't even think. She needed a cup of coffee. She sighed and rubbed her eyes, then picked up the remote control.

She turned on the TV to the local news and listened as she headed into the kitchen to put on a pot of coffee. By the time she'd poured herself a cup, she heard the news anchor mention the Golden Galaxy. She hurried back into her living room and turned up the volume.

"Planned to begin today. The mayor of Waveland said that he hoped the rain would be gone by tomorrow, so that the demolition could begin. He stated his belief that cleaning up the debris from the collapsed Sky Walk would not only remove an eyesore and a dangerous temptation for children from the town, but it would also help the families of the six people killed in the tragic accident to heal."

Today was Monday! With everything that had happened, Juliana had lost track of the days. Today was the day that demolition was supposed to begin on the Sky Walk. She walked to the window and opened the blinds. Rain was pouring down in sheets. No wonder it was delayed.

She picked up her coffee cup and sipped as she changed stations, looking for more local news, but the morning programs had started. She'd probably have to wait until noon to hear anything else about the schedule for tearing down the casino.

She sat back against the couch cushions, drinking her coffee and thinking about the casino. Soon the mass of cables and steel beams that had killed her father would be gone. Thank goodness she'd gotten his things.

His things. Everything but the day planner was still in her purse. Had it only been three days ago—Friday—that she'd gone to the casino to get them? She shuddered as she thought of the steel beam that had almost hit them.

She set her coffee cup down and dug into her purse again. There was the photo album and the few sheets of paper Dawson had found stuck behind the file drawer. She set them aside and continued digging. Where were the pen set and the ring?

A little more digging turned up the pen set, but she

couldn't find the ring. She felt along the bottom of the purse but it didn't seem to be there. She started to turn her purse upside down. Then she remembered. She'd been holding it when Dawson had grabbed her and flung her to the floor inside the supply closet. She must have dropped it.

Still, just to be sure, she dumped her purse and sifted through everything. No ring.

It had to still be on the floor of the office. She walked over to the window again and peered out. Still raining, though not as hard as before. She looked at her watch. It wasn't even eleven o'clock. Dawson wouldn't call her until after two. She had more than three hours to kill.

She loaded all her stuff back into her purse and grabbed her raincoat. She had to find her dad's wedding ring. If she didn't do it today, it might be lost forever.

# Chapter Sixteen

Dawson looked at his watch again as he turned into the parking lot at Juliana's apartment complex. He'd tried to call her a couple of times already, to let her know that he'd finished with his parents early, but she hadn't answered her phone.

He drove slowly up and down the rows of cars, listening to the slap-slap of his windshield wipers and squinting against the colorless haze created by the falling rain. He didn't see her car anywhere. He activated his Bluetooth.

"Dial name," he said as he circled around and pulled into a parking space close to the front door of her apartment building.

"Please say the name," the annoyingly patient, yet cheerful, voice begged him.

"Jules."

"Dialing Jules."

Her cell phone rang seven times before it went to voice mail. "Jules, it's one-thirty. Call me," he said before cutting the connection and turning off the car. It was the third message he'd left.

Why wasn't she answering? The phone wasn't going directly to voice mail, so it wasn't turned off or out of juice.

Then his phone rang. He looked at the display. Not Jules. Mack.

"Mack," he said. "What you got for me?"

"You've got to give me a raise for this."

"For what?"

"The secretary I just spent a great mini-vacation with? The secretary to the vice president for *finance*."

"Yeah?" Dawson pushed. He didn't have time to hear about Mack's escapades. "Give me the short version. I've got a situation here."

"Right," Mack replied, suddenly all business. "One of Heidi's jobs is payroll."

"Heidi," Dawson broke in. "Seriously?"

"Yeah. Heidi. Anyway, the checks for Bayside Industries are drawn on a bank in the Caymans."

"They're in Switzerland, and their payroll comes from the Caymans?" Dawson asked.

"Yeah, but that's not all. She got the wrong checks once. They were for a corporation based in Waveland, Mississippi."

Dawson straightened in his seat. Anticipation burned along his nerve endings. "What corporation?"

Mack paused for effect. "Meadow Gold."

A chill ran down Dawson's spine. "You're telling me that Meadow Gold and Bayside Industries use the same bank in the Caymans?"

"Not just the same bank, boss. The same account."

Dawson was afraid to breathe. He didn't want to ask the next question. Didn't want the answer to be no. "Do you have proof?"

"You'd better believe it. I have photocopies in my hot little hands."

"Photocopies?"

"When it happened, Heidi got worried that if the bank could make that kind of mistake, something might happen one day that might implicate her. She never wanted to handle payroll in the first place. So when the checks came in, she photocopied all of them plus the envelope and put them in a personal safe-deposit box, along with photocopies of Bayside Industries checks and their envelope. She also wrote out a statement about what happened and had it notarized."

"You've got copies of all of that?"

"Yep. And I should be back there by tomorrow morning."

"Call me when you touch down."

He hung up. He had the connection between Meadow Gold and Bayside Industries. The missing piece that connected Tito Vega with Meadow Gold, the company that funded the Golden Galaxy Casino. Was he one step closer to proving that Vega ordered Knoblock to skimp on the Sky Walk? He didn't know. But the papers Mack was bringing back should be enough to get a court order to open those Cayman Island bank records.

He'd parked while talking to Mack. Now he vaulted up the steps to her apartment two at a time and banged on her door. "Jules?" he called. "Juliana? Open up. It's me. I've been trying to call you."

Nothing. He held his breath and listened. He could hear the TV. She must be home. Why wasn't she answering? With worry twisting his insides, he took his phone out and dialed her number. Within a second, he heard it ringing— from inside the apartment. If she was in there, something was wrong.

"Jules!" he shouted, banging on the door.

"Hey!" a man said from behind him. Dawson whirled. A middle-aged unshaven man in a white sleeveless undershirt stuck his nose out from the apartment directly opposite Juliana's. "Shut up out here. I'm trying to sleep."

Inclining his head a fraction of an inch, Dawson turned back to Juliana's door. The man cursed and slammed his door.

He held up his key chain and chose the brightest, newest key. Thank God he'd ducked out and had a copy of Juliana's key made while she was in the hospital. If he kicked the door in, the neighbor would probably call the police. He inserted the key into the lock and turned the knob. Stepping into her living room, he closed the door behind him. "Jules?" he called, but he knew without checking that she wasn't there. The apartment felt empty.

He looked around for the remote, prepared to turn the TV off, but if Juliana—budding private investigator—came home and didn't hear it, she might think someone had broken into her apartment. So he left it on.

He surveyed the living room. School yearbooks and loose papers were spread out on the coffee table, along with a pile of small notebooks. A coffee cup was sitting precariously on the edge of the table. He picked it up. It was cold. He frowned and hit redial on his phone. When he heard her ring, he followed the sound and found her phone stuck between two couch cushions. He picked it up and pocketed it.

Damn it. She knew better than to leave without checking that she had her phone. Wherever she was, she didn't have a way to call for help. He didn't like that one bit.

Hoping that leaving the TV on meant she was on a quick errand and would be back in a few minutes, he sat down on the couch. Until she came back or he figured out where she was, he might as well do something productive. He did his best to ignore his instinct, which was telling him that she'd taken off on her own to check out whatever she'd called him about.

He looked at the books and papers spread out on the coffee table. The proof she'd mentioned that Tito Vega and her father were connected?

Without moving them, a habit he'd cultivated for his job, he studied the open books. As he'd first thought, they were yearbooks—old ones. The first one was open to the first-grade class photos. His eyes automatically skimmed the names until he came to the *C*s. There she was. Caprese.

"I'll be damned," he whispered. Juliana was skinny and had her hair pulled back in a ponytail. A huge gap-toothed grin stretched her mouth and her dark eyes danced with mischief. Dawson smiled and touched the picture. Then he shook his head and turned to the second yearbook.

It was open to the sixth-grade class photos. There was Juliana again. Her smile wasn't as natural or as mischievous, and her hair hung down to her shoulders. She had on eye makeup and lipstick and she looked like what she was—a little girl playing dress-up. He remembered her telling him that her mother had died when she was a toddler and her father had raised her.

Somewhere between sixth grade and now, she'd figured out how strikingly beautiful she was, and had learned how to make the most of her many assets.

Dawson blinked and realized the sixth-grade picture was a blur. He'd drifted off into a daydream about Juliana's long black hair and snapping dark eyes.

He rubbed a hand down his face, then slid the third yearbook out from under the second one. He compared the dates. This was Juliana's seventh-grade yearbook.

He paged through it until he found the seventh-grade class photos and there she was. Her eye makeup—if she had any on—was subtly applied and she didn't have on lipstick. *Much better,* he thought.

He sat back against the couch cushions and regarded the three books. Why had she been so adamant about retrieving them from her dad's house? What was so important about those three pages? He didn't have a clue.

He turned his attention to the small leather notebooks lying open, facedown on the table. He picked up the top one, the 2006 one, and quickly scanned the two facing pages. The dates were April 19 and 20 of this year. Then, even though he already knew who the pocket calendar belonged to, he flipped to the inside front page.

Sure enough, printed in a neat, precise hand, was the name Vincent Caprese. He went back to the page for April 20.

On the 2:00 p.m. line, he saw what Juliana had seen. A note her father wrote about Vega.

*Vega came through. Surprise! Got call from Meadow Gold Corp. Golden Galaxy, here I come! Opening June 1. Short notice...*

That's what Juliana had told him on the phone. Vega had hired her father to manage the Golden Galaxy Casino. It was another piece of information that linked Vega to Meadow Gold Corporation.

He remembered what else she'd said. *Somehow all this is connected, but I can't put it together on my own.* That's why she'd called him.

As angry as she'd been at him for lying to her about who he was, she'd turned to him first when she needed help. And he'd blown her off. He blew out an exasperated breath. His parents had been grateful that he'd gone with them to review and sign their statements, but they'd have understood if he'd told them that he had to follow up a lead on the vandals who'd thrown the Molotov cocktail.

He could have been here for Jules. He *should* have.

He frowned at the yearbooks, trying to think the way she would. Why had she pulled out old grade-school yearbooks? What could be in them that could help her with her case?

He did not have a clue, but because she'd thought they were important, he decided to go over each page thoroughly. By the time he'd gotten to the last row of names, he was more confused than ever.

Then he zeroed in on the last name and the last picture. *Anthony Vega.* Dawson knew from his own research that Vega had two children—a daughter and a son. He didn't remember their names, but there was something about the son. Hadn't he gone to prison?

Dawson looked at Juliana's sixth-grade class photos. There Anthony Vega was again. But he wasn't in the seventh-grade yearbook. So Tito Vega's son had gone to school with Juliana from first to sixth grades.

So what?

Now he understood what she'd meant when she'd said that she was sure all this was connected, but that she couldn't figure it out. He felt the same way. There was something important here, if he could just put it together.

Tito Vega got Vincent Caprese the position of casino manager with Meadow Gold Corporation, who owned the Golden Galaxy Casino. Vega's son went to grade school with Caprese's daughter. Michael Delancey was convinced that Vega was behind the collapse of the Sky Walk. What was the missing link?

He pulled out his phone. It was a smartphone but he'd rarely used all the features. But now he wanted to see what the story was with Vega's son. With a few clicks, he was on his browser, searching for Vittorio Vega. There wasn't much. At the top of Vega's bio on his real-estate webpage was a family portrait, but there was no mention of the children's names.

Dawson searched the name Anthony Vega. He got over a hundred thousand hits. He added Mississippi to the search. That brought the number down a bit. When he added the word *prison,* he finally found a small archived Mississippi newspaper article that mentioned Anthony Vega. He'd been indicted and convicted of extortion in 2008. Dawson searched further, but nothing else came up.

There was only one thing to do. He called Ryker. "What's up?" he asked when his brother answered.

"Me," Ryker said disgustedly, "to my neck in paperwork. Did Mom and Dad get their statements signed?"

"Yep. They're back at the hotel fretting about when they can go home. I need you to do something for me."

"As long as it's legal."

"Anthony Vega. What do you know about him?" While he talked, Dawson flipped through Caprese's day planner for 2006, skimming the entries. Luckily, Caprese's handwriting was neat and easy to read.

"Tito's kid? I believe he got a nickel for extortion, despite his daddy's best efforts. He was a floor manager at a casino and was hitting up players who weren't there with their wives. Seems to me he was killed in prison. Some kind of scuffle or lover's quarrel."

"That's what I thought. Got any idea when that was?"

"Hang on."

Dawson heard the soft stutter of fingers on a keyboard.

"Here it is," Ryker said. "He went to prison in 2008. He was killed sixteen months later."

"What about the name of the casino?" Dawson asked.

"It's right here—yeah. The Beachview Casino in Gulfport."

At that exact moment Dawson's gaze lit on Anthony Vega's name, printed in Caprese's neat handwriting. "Great. Thanks," he said.

"What are you up to, Daw? You're not going to tangle with Tito Vega, are you?"

"I've got a theory. If it's right, then I may know who killed Vincent Caprese and five other innocent people."

"Do me a favor, maverick. Call the police. Don't go up against Vega by yourself."

"Do *me* a favor and tell me why nobody has put him away before now."

Ryker sighed. "You know what Con Delancey always said. *Politics and crime are like love and marriage.*"

"Right," Dawson put in sarcastically. "You can't have one without the other. Tell that to Aunt Bettye."

"It's just a saying, Daw."

"Don't tell me you buy into that?"

"Luckily, I don't have to worry about Vega. His influence doesn't reach as far as Chef Voleur. He concentrates on the Mississippi Gulf Coast."

"Lucky you."

"Just watch out, Daw. You mess with Vega and somebody's going to get hurt."

"You know, nobody has messed with Vega so far, and it looks like a lot of people are getting hurt." Dawson thought about the threat Vega had sent his dad. "Dad ever mention anything about Vega to you?"

"Dad? No. Why?"

Dawson didn't want to go into it. If Michael had thought Ryker or Reilly could do anything, he'd have told them about the threat on his wife's life. "Nothing. Something I was thinking about. I've got to go," he said. "Talk to you later."

"Daw, be careful."

"Always am," Dawson tossed back, then hung up. He read Caprese's note written on April 6, in his 2006 day planner.

*Anthony Vega. Flr mgr hired 01/2006. Q re: blackmail! Davis interviewing complainants.*

Anthony Vega worked for Caprese in 2006! He turned to the front of the day planner. On the inside front cover Caprese had printed his name and his position. *General manager, Beachview Casino, 3700 Beach Blvd, Gulfport, Mississippi.*

*This* was the missing piece of information that Jules was working on. Vincent Caprese had hired Anthony Vega as a floor manager at the Beachview Casino. Dawson glanced at the yearbooks. Maybe because Vega had claimed to be a friend of Juliana?

He flipped through the pages and found more notes about Anthony Vega's illegal activities. Finally on September 10, 2006, Vincent Caprese had Anthony Vega arrested for extortion.

It was motive for Tito Vega. Caprese had sent his son to prison and the son had died there. Dawson stuck the day planner in his pocket to give to Detective Hardy. This really could be the missing piece that could end up linking Vega to Juliana's father's death.

Dawson looked at his watch. "Damn it," he muttered. "Where are you, Jules?" The clock in his phone read three-fifteen. He'd been here over an hour, and she knew he was going to call her after two o'clock. Hadn't she realized she didn't have her phone with her?

He'd go after her—if he had a clue where she'd gone. He looked at the rest of the items on the coffee table. It appeared she'd left in a hurry. What had she been looking at besides the yearbooks and day planners?

Among the items on the coffee table were the things she'd pulled out of her dad's desk at the casino. The loose paper and torn file folder he'd pulled from the back of the desk, the pen set and the photograph album. He skimmed the loose pages. They were an original and a copy of a routine memo to the Golden Galaxy administrative staff. No help there.

He dismissed the pen set Jules had found in Caprese's desk drawer, and although he wanted to look at them, he also dismissed the collection of photos in the leather pocket-size photo album.

Wasn't there something else she'd found? She'd felt around the back of the drawers, searching for anything of her father's.

Then he remembered. The last thing she'd found was the

wedding ring. She'd had it in her fist when the beam had come crashing down. Only Dawson's quick instinctive reaction had saved them.

Oh, crap. It wasn't here with the rest of the things she'd brought with her from her dad's office. Had she dropped it when the beam fell?

Something from the TV drew his attention. He looked up. The news anchor was announcing the top stories of the day. With a still photo from the Golden Galaxy Casino pictured behind her, she announced that because of the rain, demolition and cleanup from the collapse of the Sky Walk would be delayed until the next day, Tuesday.

"Ah, hell, Jules," Dawson muttered. She'd gone there. He knew it as surely as he knew his own name. She'd gone back to the site of her dad's death and her own near-death experience to retrieve her dad's ring.

JULIANA SNEEZED into the crook of her arm. Her eyes itched and her throat was getting scratchy from the dust and debris. She was never going to find her dad's ring. It was after three-thirty and the sun was low enough that her dad's office was cloaked in shadow. She continued her methodical search of the supply closet, thankful the beam that had nearly hit them had been removed.

She blinked. Was that a glint of metal? It was, but she'd unearthed a pile of nails and screws that had reflected the beam of her flashlight. This was probably another one.

Crouching down, she held the light steady, moving it a fraction of an inch at a time, as she tried to catch the metallic glint again. There it was. She reached out, but it was just a tiny piece of aluminum foil—a candy wrapper?

She was about ready to give up and get out of the dark deserted building. From the moment she'd come in through the main entrance and discovered that the electricity was off, she'd felt like ghosts were breathing down her neck. As she'd made her way past the silent slot machines, she remembered the first time she'd sneaked in here on Friday, three days ago, looking for her dad's things. The machines had lined up in front of her like grim soldiers guarding the dead, their pull levers sticking up like rifles. And that had been with lights on.

Today they were much more ominous. She'd cringed as she'd hurried past them, the beam of her flashlight sending shadows dancing and her imagination spinning out of control. Every glass screen looked like a monster's face in the stark flashlight's glow. Sometimes from the corner of her eye, she thought she'd seen them move.

She'd been practically running by the time she'd reached the office. It hadn't helped that for every step she'd taken, she'd been sure she heard footsteps behind her.

Even now, creaks and rattles and rustling noises plagued her ears. Were other precarious beams working loose from their bolts? Rats and cockroaches? Ghosts?

Another creepy sound swirled around her. She hoped it was the wind, but it sounded like people whispering. The susurrous mutterings rose then faded, rose then faded. It had to be the wind, didn't it? Human beings' whispers wouldn't fade in and out. Juliana shivered and ran a hand across the back of her neck where she could swear she felt a cold breath.

*We know there's nobody there,* her little voice assured her. *Do we?* she countered. She set her jaw and concentrated on searching the dirty floor.

The flashlight's beam glinted again. This time the flash was definitely yellow rather than silver. Carefully, she slid her hand down the beam of light, and patted the small circle of illumination on the floor.

She felt something. Swallowing the hope that sprang up to clog her throat, she closed her fingers around the hard, circular object and stood. Without daring to breathe, she shone the light on her fist and slowly opened her fingers.

She'd found it. Her dad's ring! The wedding band he'd worn for years until it became too small. She held it up and blew the dust off it, then shone the light on the engraving inside the gold band.

*Love forever, J.*

Her dad had told her the story of their wedding many times. Her mother, Julia Mills Caprese, had placed it on her dad's finger the day they were married. Her dad had given Juliana her mother's ring when she'd graduated from high school. It was in her safe-deposit box. She carefully tucked her dad's ring into the pocket of her jeans.

As she turned to look at the wreck of her dad's office, where he'd drawn his last breath, more creaks and thuds echoed through the main floor of the casino. She needed to get out of here before the sun went down and left the casino pitch-dark.

Her flashlight had fresh batteries, but the place was giving her the creeps.

She picked her way back to the door of the office and turned toward the main entrance. The day was cloudy, but a dull gray light shown in from the glass doors. The dim glow reflecting off the slot machines played tricks on her vision. She was sure she could see them moving, marching in sync, guarding the doors. She shivered. If only they were guards, keeping her safe.

Then she saw a different movement, a paler, slimmer shadow among the one-armed bandits. She blinked and looked again, but it was still there.

Suddenly, a light flashed. Her heart jumped into her throat and lodged there, interfering with her breathing. She gasped and gasped again, her breaths sawing loudly.

*Get a grip!* she commanded herself. *Breathe slowly, evenly, silently.*

The light was still there, glaring in her eyes. She squinted and saw the pale halo around the bright circle of light. It was a flashlight. Her heart jumped again, thudding against her chest wall and pounding in her ears.

Who was it? The beam flared as the person swung it from side to side. He was just inside the main entrance, probably sixty or more feet away from her.

Then the pattern of light changed. He was coming toward her. Her hand went to her throat and she could feel her pulse throbbing rapidly. She squinted again, but whoever it was, he'd walked out of the light from the glass doors and all she could see was the flashlight's beam.

Maybe it was Dawson, she told herself. But she knew it wasn't. That pale shadow looked nothing like his long, lean body. Plus, he would have already identified himself to her. In fact, he'd already be berating her, telling her that if she wanted to be a private investigator, she needed to learn how to hide in plain sight.

The police, she thought. It had to be the police. She sniffed in irritation. Were they watching the abandoned casino 24/7? But as the light came closer and she had to strain to hear the almost-silent pad of footsteps, she knew it wasn't the police, either. They wouldn't be sneaking up on her. They'd have their high-intensity flashlights next to their raised weapons and be shouting at her to put her hands up and freeze.

Whoever was behind that beam of light had no more business being in the abandoned casino than she did. Had they come here to find something they'd lost, like she had?

Or were they here for her?

## Chapter Seventeen

Juliana reached into her purse for her phone, but it wasn't in the pocket where she usually kept it. She felt frantically around the bottom where things tended to collect, but no luck. Then she remembered calling Dawson on it. She'd set it down on the coffee table or on the couch. How stupid of her to leave without checking that she had it.

She was on her own. Her pulse throbbed in her throat—those footsteps were coming for her. She could hear Dawson's voice in her head. *I told you to stay put.*

*Damn it, Dawson. If you'd made time for me, I might not be here with faceless people coming at me in the dark.* Her hand went to the small of her back, to her weapon tucked into the waistband of her jeans.

*Put that gun away. If you want to be a private investigator, you've got to know when to attack and when to hide,* Dawson's voice told her.

*Fine.* This was definitely the time to hide. If she turned off her flashlight and didn't run into anything, she might be able to slip out through the west side fire door before her pursuer could get to her.

She pressed the off switch. The click was alarmingly loud in the suddenly pitch-black silence. The only thing she could see was the flashlight beam approaching. It stopped and wavered, then the person holding it lifted it and swung it in a wide arc, as if trying to find her.

She shrank back against the wall. Without her flashlight, she felt disoriented. Without the wall, she'd certainly lose her balance and fall. It was an awful feeling. She blinked hard, as if blinking would help her eyes to adapt. The sun peeking through the windows barely spread a dusty sheen over the wreckage. Rather than helping, the dim glow actually hurt. The shadows seemed blacker, and the light kept her eyes from adjusting.

The flashlight kept coming. She needed to get to the fire exit. That was her only chance of escape. It was to the left of her dad's office door. If she worked her way to her left while hugging the left wall, maybe she could make it without tripping over anything.

She inched her way along the wall, which had survived most of the damage when the Sky Walk collapsed. Shuffling, sliding her sneaker-clad feet carefully along the Italian tiles, she moved slowly, feeling for objects or debris that might trip her up. She kept her eyes on the flashlight beam coming toward her.

He had slowed down. Why? Whoever he was, he'd had plenty of time to get to her by now. She clung to the wall, her left hand feeling the way ahead of her.

Her hand hit something cold and hard with a dull thud that to her ears sounded like a gong. She felt it—it was a fire extinguisher. She must be close to the door. She blew out a breath she hadn't realized she'd been holding. Her stuttering pulse slowed.

The flashlight's beam swept across the floor, pulling her gaze to it. She measured the near edge of the ellipse with her eyes. He was close and he was still coming.

Then a muffled sound reverberated through the building.

Panic gripped her again and she froze. Her fingers tingled and her stomach sank.

The sound was unmistakable, wasn't it? It sounded like a heavy door closing, she thought. But where? In front of her?

The echo bounced from wall to wall, from ceiling to floor, all around her. Why did sounds that were ordinary in the daytime become magnified and distorted in the dark?

Taking a deep breath and blowing it out eased her shivering panic a bit. *Concentrate. Listen.*

Who had slammed the door, if it was a door slamming? It could have been a piece of debris falling, she supposed. Did the guy with the flashlight have a partner? A dreaded certainty weighed her down. Even if the sound she'd heard had come from the fire exit, she still had only one choice. She had to get to the door. She didn't know how far the nearest exit was and she'd never find it in the dark.

With her tense muscles beginning to ache and her confidence draining away, she slid farther along the wall.

Her toe bumped something. It rolled noisily. She stiffened, her arms and legs quivering in reaction. Her first instinct was to reach for it, to quiet it, but she suppressed the urge. The man with the flashlight knew where she was anyway.

*We've got to keep going. Get outside where we can see.* It sounded so easy, but what if she opened the door to an ambush?

A chill crawled up her spine, raising the hairs on her nape. Her body was betraying her—giving in to fear. She was close to the breaking point.

Suddenly, she was surrounded by sound. Rustling, whispering. The nearly silent footsteps were getting louder. The flashlight's beam was brighter—blinding. And the sound of that door still resonated through the walls.

Forcing herself to ignore her imagination, she patted the wall with her left hand and stretched to feel as far in front of her as possible. Where was the damn fire door? Shouldn't she have reached it long before now?

She kept moving, her hand kept sliding until finally her fingers hit a door frame. Thank God!

At the same time, the flashlight beam reached her boots. This was it. She pulled her weapon from the waistband of her jeans, thumbed off the safety and gripped it two-handed.

She took a deep breath and pushed against the metal panic bar with her elbow, preparing to lead with her gun. Maybe they wouldn't expect her to have a weapon.

The door slammed open. Light blinded her. Her grip tightened on her gun. Then she felt a rough hand on her arm and pain exploded behind her eyes.

JULIANA'S HEAD FELT LIKE somebody had stomped on it. She curled her fingers and they scraped across rough, cold concrete. She decided that before she moved, she needed to do an inventory—see if she was all in one piece. She knew her head was attached to her neck because both of them throbbed with pain.

Her shoulders hurt, too, especially the left one. She flexed her fingers against the concrete. All ten present and accounted for. She felt vaguely nauseated and her left hip ached. Apparently, she was still intact.

She tried lifting her head. The throbbing pain turned to screaming agony.

"All right, then. Stop whimpering and sit up slowly."

She jerked in surprise and pain stabbed into her brain. Carefully maneuvering her hands under her to lift her leaden head, she grimaced and pulled herself to her hands and knees.

"Oh!" she grunted as she rolled into a sitting position. As soon as her hands were free, she gripped either side of her head. Her fingers touched thick, sticky wetness on the left side of her head. Blood. "Ow," she groaned.

"I said, enough whining."

She raised her head a millimeter at a time. Highly polished black shoes came into her line of vision, as did two exquisitely tailored pant legs. She almost chuckled. Her brain seemed to be on autopilot. She couldn't make it assess the situation or scope out her surroundings for a possible escape. In fact, it hurt her head to even think about not thinking.

She winced and that hurt her head a lot. So she just let her thoughts go and listened to them. The tailored pant legs were a dark charcoal-gray with a pinstripe that she would swear was pink. The coat was a match for the pants. The shirt, which had to be silk, was white and the tie was an abstract pattern of gray, black, white and pink.

Then she noticed that the suit was big—very big. It had to be to fit that body into it. Those were the hands that had grabbed her—huge and beefy. He wore a large opal ring on the left pinkie and his nails were buffed.

"Feeling better?" the man asked, as he shrugged out of his suit jacket and tie and rolled up his shirt sleeves. He carefully folded the jacket and tie and set them on the loading dock.

Juliana noticed something odd about his voice. No, not his voice, his words. He had some kind of accent. She filed that information away to think about later, when her head didn't hurt so much.

She focused on his head and wished upon him the pain she was feeling in hers. He was bald—shaved-head bald, not genetically bald. His head was shaped like an egg, but he didn't look silly. He looked ominous. His eyebrows were bushy and slanted downward toward his nose, giving him a perpetual scowl. The nose looked as though it had been broken more than once. His lips were full. His mouth had an odd slant that transformed the frown into a smirk.

She shivered. He looked as though he could kill her with one hand and not even chip a nail.

"Who are you?" she demanded. Her voice gave her away, though. It was high-pitched and timid.

"Ah, the usual question. I'll take that as a yes, that you are feeling better. Shall we get down to business, then?"

She was beginning to notice things around her, although the connection between her eyes and her brain was still a bit hazy. They were right outside the west fire exit, on a concrete loading dock. Somewhere—she couldn't remember which side—there was a ramp for rolling dollies and carts. If she could get to it—

A noise behind her made her jump. The throbbing in her head made her teeth ache as she squinted at the man behind her. She recognized his skinny frame and the ridiculous tattoos he had all over his arms. He was holding a flashlight that had blood smeared on the edge of it.

"You're that guy!" she cried. "You stole my letter!" She couldn't come up with his name, but she knew it was him. She recognized the colorful snake tattoo, as well as his narrow face and bad teeth.

"Get her up," the big man said.

"Maynard," she said. "Your name's Maynard."

"She's—" Maynard started.

"Shut up! Get her on her feet."

Maynard reached for her. She cringed away and held up her hands. "Don't touch me. I'll get up." She tried to get her feet under her, but her head began to swim.

Maynard grabbed her under her arms and jerked her upright.

Nausea gripped her. For a couple of seconds she clung to Maynard as she struggled to stand on her own.

"Very good, Ms. Caprese. Now to business."

"What—business?" Juliana rasped. She let go of Maynard's ratty T-shirt and wiped her hands on her jeans. Getting away from him cured a lot of the queasiness. "Who are you?"

"It doesn't matter who I am. Not to you. What matters is why we're here like this. You're meddling in things that are none of your business."

"None of my—" Sharp, searing anger burned away her queasiness. "I am trying to find out who caused my father's death. It *is* my business!"

The bald man shook his head. He reached into the inside pocket of his coat and brought out a fingernail file. He looked at his nails, then ran the file across one. "You're annoying Mr. Vega. That's never a good thing."

"I *knew* it! Vega's behind all this, isn't he? You—" She jabbed a finger in Maynard's direction. "Vega ordered you to attack me, didn't he?"

"Please, Ms. Caprese," the bald man said, lifting the hand with the file in it. "Calm down. I'm sure you can understand that accidents happen."

Juliana's scalp burned; she was so angry. "The Sky Walk's collapse was *no* accident. It was negligence at the very least."

The man shook his head, his expression showing regret. "As I said, accidents happen. It would be a tragedy if you were to fall from the cross beams of the casino's ceiling while trying to find proof for your theory about the Sky Walk."

"What?" His words made no sense at first. *Casino's ceiling?* Her head was still pounding. Then it hit her: he was threatening her.

"Oh, no," she said, shaking her head. "You'll never get me up there. If you want me dead, you'll have to shoot me. I'm not going anywhere."

"Trust me, you will. Maynard—"

Juliana reached for her gun but slapped at her empty waistband. Maynard's skinny arm hooked around her neck with surprising strength. She instinctively grabbed his tattooed

forearm and tried to stomp on his feet, but he was as quick
and agile as he was strong.

The bald man approached her. He still held something in
his hand, but it was no longer the fingernail file. It was a syringe.

"No!" she cried, then filled her lungs to scream, but he
punched her in the stomach.

Her breath whooshed out and pain cramped her insides.
Before she could draw in another, she felt a pinprick on the
side of her neck and everything went black.


THE CORVETTE'S TIRES screeched as Dawson turned in to the
large driveway on the west end of the Golden Galaxy Casino.
He had no plan except to storm the casino and find Jules. He
headed toward the main entrance, but as he passed the loading dock, he caught a glimpse of a white face and a cloud of
black hair.

*Jules!* He slammed on the brakes. Threw the stick into
Reverse. Replayed the snapshot his brain had just taken.

A man held Jules's limp body as a smaller figure opened
the fire door.

Dawson laid rubber as he backed around the massive concrete corner of the loading platform. Screeching to a halt and
killing the engine, he jumped out just as the smaller man
whirled around in the doorway to look at him. It was Maynard, the skinny tattooed skunk who'd attacked Jules and
stolen her letter.

The skunk's close-set eyes widened. He yelled something.
Then he backed through the door and manually jerked it shut.

Dawson took a running start and leaped up onto the dock.
He lunged for the door. Pulling his weapon with one hand,
he yanked the door open with the other.

He forced himself to enter cautiously. One or both men
might be on the other side, waiting to shoot him. Standing in

the doorway, he was painfully aware that his form was clearly outlined by the waning daylight. But he needed the light, too. He'd be totally blind in the dark until his eyes adapted—a sitting duck.

He didn't see anyone, but he heard footsteps—the sound of leather-soled shoes on hollow metal—the sound moving upward. Could that be what it sounded like? A ladder? He hadn't noticed a metal ladder in the casino. It had to be a service ladder, leading up to the network of beams that formed the framework of the huge glass dome. Was the bald goon climbing up to the rafter beams? With Jules?

Dawson gripped his weapon two-handed and swept the area in front of him with his gaze, then he let the fire door close.

When the sound of the latch slipping into place echoed through the dark building, he blinked several times. *Come on. I need to see.*

He heard the bullet whiz past him at the same time as the report. He ducked, too late to dodge that bullet. But he had to shield himself from the next.

Maynard had to be as blinded by the darkness as he. If so, he'd lucked out with a damn close shot. But just in case the skunk could see better than he could, he stayed low, studying the shadows, trying to judge what was where by the different shades of black.

He remembered that the poker room was on this end of the casino, near Caprese's office. Now the varied shadows made a little more sense. They were oval tables and straight chairs and small beverage carts. Plenty of cover. Or they would be once he figured out where Maynard was. He had an inkling from that first shot, but if the little skunk was smarter than Dawson thought he was, he'd have moved after he fired.

Crouched against the wall, Dawson yanked out his phone. He dialed 9-1-1.

"This is 9-1-1. What is the nature of your emergency?" the detached voice asked.

"Golden Galaxy Casino, Waveland," he said quietly but distinctly. "Shots fired. Two armed males holding female hostage."

"Sir, can you—"

A shot rang out.

"Send the police now! Golden Galaxy!" he commanded and hung up. He stuck the phone back in his pocket.

"Maynard!" he shouted. "Give it up. You know I'll get you."

No response. Would Maynard figure out Dawson was baiting him? Dawson was betting he wouldn't.

"I'd hate to have to kill you, Maynard. Give yourself up and I'll put in a good word for you."

"Screw you!" Maynard shouted in his tinny voice.

Dawson pinpointed the direction. For a split second, he hesitated. How much was he willing to bet that the big man had carried Jules up to the metal beams? How much was he willing to bet that she wasn't there with Maynard?

Was he willing to bet her life?

"Jules!" he shouted, but there was no answer. He shook his head. He had to. It was the only chance he had to save her. If he was wrong and his bullet found her— He shuddered. He took a long breath, rose and fired a shot.

Maynard yelped, cursed, then returned fire—three shots.

He doubted he'd hit the skinny skunk. The yelp was more likely surprise. He held his fire and crawled out onto the floor, away from the wall.

Another shot rang out. He dived instinctively and slammed into the leg of a table. He rubbed his stinging arm, feeling the unmistakable thick warmth of blood. The damn thing had cut him. It was metal, and that was a good thing. He was glad to sacrifice a little blood to find out that the tables would shield him from bullets. Now if he could just get Maynard to empty his gun. So far he'd fired four rounds.

"Maynard, you're going to run out of bullets," he shouted, hoping the skunk wouldn't be able to keep from bragging if he had another magazine.

No answer.

Dawson wasted another bullet, hoping to draw Maynard's fire. Sure enough, two more shots rang out.

Then, just as the echo of the second shot was fading, Dawson heard a sound that chilled him to the bone.

Jules screaming—or trying to.

## Chapter Eighteen

Juliana had tried to scream, but her voice sounded so weak that it broke and ended with a fading moan.

"Jules!" he cried, unable to help himself. Where was she? The sound had echoed through the silent casino, but Dawson was pretty sure it had originated from over his head. That bald goon *had* carried her up to the ceiling. But why?

*Bald goon.* Damn! It was the same man who'd threatened his dad, who'd threatened his mom's life. He worked for Tito Vega!

So it was Vega who'd had her followed, who was determined to stop her from digging into the collapse of the Sky Walk.

"Daw—" Jules started, but Dawson heard a sharp slap and she cried out. The bastard had hit her. Anger burned in him.

*Stop,* he ordered himself. *Focus.* What was Vega up to?

Then he knew. Oh, God! He knew without a doubt exactly what the plan was. The goon had taken her up to the metal framework that had held the Sky Walk suspended over the casino.

It was brilliant. He had to give Vega that. *Poor Juliana had become obsessed with finding someone to blame for her father's death. She'd climbed up there to see for herself if the Sky Walk had failed or had been tampered with. She'd slipped and fallen to her death on the floor of the casino.*

Dawson shook off that image and tamped down the fear and sudden grief that came with it. He couldn't let emotions get in the way if he was going to have any chance to save her.

Tomorrow when demolition started, if the work crew didn't find her broken body in the wreckage, they'd plow her under the twisted wires and debris.

"Hey, Maynard, why did your fat, ugly partner leave you down here to get shot? Because if you don't give up now and make a deal, I *am* going to shoot you. And because you hurt her, I'm going to make it count. How'd you like to get gut shot? You'll have to carry your bathroom around strapped to a hole in your belly for the rest of your life. How much fun do you think that'll be in prison?"

"Shut up!" Maynard shrieked.

At the same time, the bald goon yelled, "Maynard, he's trying to rattle you! Kill him and get up here!"

Dawson rose up enough to get off a shot, then he scrambled toward the stage. He was gambling that the service ladder was hidden behind the stage.

Maynard shot three more times. Hell, that was nine shots. How big a magazine did he have? Must be a fifteen or a twenty-five round.

Dawson craned his neck, trying to get a glimpse of Jules and the goon. The sun was long gone and he could see the dark sky through the glass dome above him.

"Hey, Baldy," he shouted, squinting, searching for a human shape.

There! He saw a movement. Then he could make out Jules's pale oval face and the goon's shiny head. "You're not leaving here alive, you know."

"Don't worry about me," the man yelled. "Worry about yourself and your young woman. You are the ones who won't leave here alive."

"How're you going to get out? The police are on their way,

and of course I'm here, just waiting for you to climb down those stairs." Dawson heard a noise behind him and ducked. He felt the heat from the bullet as it whizzed past his neck. Way too close for comfort.

Maynard had decided to go on the offensive. He'd picked up a piece of plastic from the front of a slot machine and was using it as a shield as he walked toward Dawson. He fired again. *Twelve.* Did he have three more bullets or thirteen?

Dawson hit the floor and rolled under one of the game tables. He tipped it over. Maynard put three bullets into the tabletop.

"Enough of this," Dawson muttered. He didn't care if Maynard had ten bullets left. Rising from behind the table, Dawson took aim and shot Maynard, right through the plastic shield. He hit him in the gut, just like he'd promised.

Maynard screamed.

Dawson quickly went over and grabbed Maynard's gun. "You pitiful idiot," he said. "Your damn shield was plastic, you imbecile."

Maynard was sobbing and moaning. "D-deal—" he gasped.

"Not now." Dawson turned his back on Maynard and maneuvered between tables until he was less than six feet away from the ladder. He shone his flashlight up and found them.

The goon had his forearm around her neck. It looked like her feet were barely touching the ground. Whenever he wanted to, Baldy could let go and with no more than a nudge, could send Jules crashing to the casino floor. And there was nothing Dawson could do. The most he could hope for would be to put himself under her, hoping to break her fall. But from fifty feet, he doubted either one of them would survive.

He racked his brain but couldn't think of a way to save her. He'd promised to protect her. He could hear her now.

*I can take care of myself.* His mouth turned up in a smile, then it hit him.

She could save herself. She might end up falling anyway, or Baldy could toss her over. But it was her only chance to live.

"Jules, listen to me," he shouted. "Grab hold of him. His arm, his neck, his belt. Anything you can grab. You've got only one chance, so make it good. Hold on and don't let go. No matter what! Then kick him, bite him. But *don't let go.* If you do, you'll fall. I'm coming up." He headed for the metal ladder. He had to hand it to Baldy. He'd climbed up here one-handed, carrying Jules. While she was slender, she was tall and shapely—certainly not tiny. The man must be strong.

"Maynard! You stupid—" Baldy broke off and growled.

Dawson could barely see the two of them, but he could hear Jules grunting and Baldy growling and cursing. He almost lost his grip—his hands were trembling so. *Don't fall, Jules. I can't lose you.*

"Maynard, shoot him!"

Dawson laughed out loud. "Maynard can't shoot, Baldy. Why don't you do your own dirty work?" The thought had barely popped into his head before he'd said it. He was sure Baldy had a gun. Maybe he'd pull it and try to shoot Dawson. If Dawson could make him do that, it would make it even harder for him to hold on to Jules.

"Ah!" Jules shrieked.

Dawson's heart nearly exploded with panic. He was almost at the top of the stairs, but he'd had to use both hands to climb. He paused to pull his gun out of his waistband.

Baldy was turning in place, trying to maintain his balance while kicking and swinging at Jules. Somehow she'd managed to grab on to the back of his belt. Her legs were wrapped around his knees. She was desperately holding on as Baldy whirled and grabbed at her clothes, her hair, anything he could reach.

He snagged her hair and pulled. Jules shrieked and almost lost her grip.

"Freeze, Baldy," Dawson shouted as he stepped onto the two-foot-wide beam from the ladder. It was amazing that the man could stay on these beams, as big as he was.

The bald goon cursed and spat, then he let go of Jules's hair and reached inside his coat.

"Don't do it!" Dawson warned.

Baldy ignored him. His hand came out holding his weapon, a big 9 mm. But instead of aiming it at Dawson, he put the barrel of the gun against Jules's thigh.

Dawson's pulse burned through his veins like jet fuel. Had he blown Jules's only chance? "Wait!" he yelled. "What do you want?"

Baldy smiled. "You are smarter than I thought. That's good. I want out of here, free and clear, of course."

"Can't do that," Dawson said, trying to keep the fear out of his voice. "But I can let you out alive. If you shoot her, I swear I'll make you a quadriplegic."

Baldy shook his head. "You're not going to risk shooting me. If I go down, so does your girlfriend."

"I can get you a deal. I've got influence," Dawson pressed.

"Not good enough." Baldy had the barrel of the gun pressed against the top of Jules's right thigh, which was wrapped around his knees. His elbow was bent and he held the barrel straight, to keep from accidentally hitting himself with the bullet. "Try again."

Dawson saw Jules bow her head. Was she losing her grip on Baldy? Were her arms and legs getting tired? *Don't give up.*

"Come on, man. Vega would give you up in a heartbeat.

Give me Vega and I'm betting you could skate by with five years, no more."

"I can't be in prison," Baldy protested. "I might as well die right here." He looked down at his gun, as if contemplating taking his life.

At that instant, Jules leaned farther over, let go of Baldy's belt with her right hand. In one fluid motion she grabbed his shirt sleeve, opened her mouth and bit down on the skin of his elbow with all her might.

Baldy bellowed, jerked sharply and nearly dropped his gun. He teetered for a second or two, and nearly fell when Jules let go of his belt and scrambled away. But he finally managed to grab hold of a strut.

"Careful, Jules!" Dawson shouted as he dived toward her across the metal latticework.

Baldy touched his elbow. His hand came away covered in blood. He roared in rage. "You—" he growled at Jules. He lifted his arm and aimed at her.

"Jules!" Dawson yelled. He threw himself in front of her, grabbing a wire to steady himself and, in the same motion, he raised his gun to shoot.

Something struck him right below his ribs. The impact knocked him backward. The wire cut into his hand. He fired at Baldy one-handed, too off-balance to aim.

He heard the man grunt, heard his leather-soled shoes slipping on the metal.

*Don't fall, man! Don't die.* They needed his testimony.

"Police," a commanding voice rang out from below them. "You up there, drop the gun."

Dawson was shocked. He hadn't heard sirens. He'd decided the 9-1-1 operator had written him off as a crank call, and he hadn't had a chance to call back. He blew out a breath of relief, which hurt—a lot.

He touched the place where it hurt and his hand came

away all bloody. Had he been shot? It didn't matter. Everything was okay now. The cavalry had arrived. He kept Baldy in his sights, just to be sure he obeyed the officer.

"I said drop it," the officer yelled. "I *will* shoot you." Dawson had no doubt he would. His determination resounded in his voice.

Baldy looked at the gun and Dawson's heart rate tripled. His mouth had lost its perpetual sneer. He looked like—like he was considering suicide. Dawson took a breath to try to reason with him.

Then Baldy met his gaze. "Deal?" he said.

Dawson nodded. "Deal."

"This is your last warning, mister," the officer shouted.

"Don't shoot. I'm dropping the gun," Baldy yelled. "Here it comes." He let go of the weapon. It hit the marble floor with a sharp clatter.

Then two officers were scrambling up the metal ladder and heading straight for Baldy. They warned him to stand still while they patted him down and cautioned him to walk carefully on the beams and not make any sudden moves.

"You go down the ladder first," one officer told him. "Sergeant Flynn has you covered. Flynn, coming down," he shouted.

As Baldy climbed down, Dawson could hear Flynn reciting his Miranda rights.

The officer turned toward him. "You all right? Any injuries?"

Dawson shifted and grimaced. "I've got a flesh wound, but—"

"Ma'am, are you okay?" the officer called to Jules.

She didn't answer.

"Jules?" Dawson whirled in place. She was lying still—too still. Her eyes were closed.

"Jules, answer me!" He touched her shoulder but she didn't

move. He reached out to push a strand of hair away from her face and his fingers came away wet. He stared at them, uncomprehendingly at first. Then he knew.

It was blood—her blood.


JULIANA WOKE UP but she wished she hadn't. The lights were too bright and something was buzzing around her head. She lay there without moving, hoping she could go back to sleep. And maybe she could, if her head weren't hurting so badly.

The buzzing wasn't helping, either. She tried to block it out, but it just got louder and more annoying.

*...still not talking...*

*...if he'll give up Vega or not...*

Those were words, mixed in with the buzzing. Giving up on the possibility of any more sleep, Juliana lay there listening. She'd recognized some of the words, so maybe if she lay very still, she'd be able to make sense of all of them.

*...when she wakes up enough to...*

That was Dawson. "Daw—" She opened her eyes, blinked and looked around. Moving her eyes made her head hurt, so she closed them again.

"She's awake."

"Ms. Caprese, I just need to—"

"Hey, Brian!" Dawson's voice again, sharp and commanding. "Get out. I promise you'll get to talk to her, but not now. Go put the screws to your Mr. Schumer again."

Juliana left her eyes closed. She listened to the people leaving. After the footsteps faded, she heard a door close, then Dawson took her hand in his.

She squinted at him.

"How're you feeling?" he asked.

She narrowed her gaze. Why was he being so nice? A knife blade of fear tore through her and she gasped.

"What is it?" he asked, squeezing her hand more tightly. "Are you hurting?"

"What happened?" she asked. "I can't remember—"

"You were at the Golden Galaxy and two men grabbed you. One was—"

Juliana didn't hear anything else Dawson said. Memories pelted her like machine gun fire, rat-tat-tatting too fast to process. All she could do was let them blast the inside of her eyelids.

The dark casino. The slot machines. The eerie sounds. Flashlight beam. Whisperings. Bald man. Syringe. Dizziness. Gunshots. Grasping. Holding on. Blood. Pain. Silence.

She pressed her palms against the side of her head. Her fingers touched a bandage. She explored it gingerly as she waited for her head to stop spinning.

"What's wrong, Jules? Is it your head? Should I call a nurse?" He reached for the call button. "Yeah, let me get a nurse."

"No!" she snapped. "Stop. Nobody else." She cautiously lowered her hands, testing to see if the machine gun fire had stopped. It had—at least for the moment.

"Tell me what happened," she ordered him.

He gave her a hard glance, then stood.

She gasped. Under the blue scrub shirt he had on, she saw the bulge of a bandage. "What's that?" she asked, pointing. "You're hurt."

He looked down and gingerly touched the bandage. "This, nothing. It's nothing."

She frowned at him. "Dawson—"

"Okay, I'll give you the abridged version for now. You apparently went to the casino to find the ring you'd dropped when the beam fell."

"How—"

He held up a hand. "Let me finish, then you can ask questions. Somehow, Maynard and Schumer cornered you and knocked you out with something—we found the syringe and it's being analyzed. Schumer carried—"

"Wait," she said, holding up a hand. "Schumer?"

"The bald goon. He carried you up to the ceiling framework. We think he was planning to push you, making it look like you'd climbed up there and lost your balance. It would have been a tragic accident and your suspicions and your proof would die with you."

"But you followed me."

Dawson shook his head. "No. You didn't wait for me, so I had to try and *guess* where you'd gone. If I'd been a few seconds later, you'd be dead."

Did she imagine it or did Dawson's voice break? "He shot you, didn't he?" she snapped. "That's a gunshot wound."

"He did." Dawson walked over to the bed and touched the bandage on her temple. "But what I didn't know, and what scared me to death, was that the bullet went through me and grazed your temple." He paused. "God, Jules, I thought—"

"Then why aren't you in bed like me? If the bullet went through you—"

A nurse who'd come in holding a clipboard interrupted. "I'll tell you why, Ms. Caprese. He's gone AMA—against medical advice. He wouldn't stay in bed. Had to get in here to see you." The nurse leveled a hard stare at Dawson, then turned back to her.

"You're being discharged. Do you have someone who can drive you home and stay with you for a couple of days?"

"She does," Dawson said quickly.

"Good. Now if you'll just sign these—" The nurse thrust the clipboard into Juliana's lap and handed her a pen. "We'll get you out of here. That first sheet is yours. It's wound care instructions. Although your little scratch won't be a problem.

Put some antibiotic ointment on it and keep it bandaged for a couple of days."

Juliana signed where she was supposed to and handed the clipboard back to the nurse. While she was signing, Dawson's phone rang. He stepped out of the room to answer it.

By the time he was done, the nurse had brought a wheelchair. While she wheeled Juliana downstairs, Dawson went ahead to bring the car around. He got her situated in the passenger seat and headed east.

"I'm taking you to my condo. You can rest while I go meet Brian Hardy. Schumer's finally decided to talk."

"No, I'm going with you," Juliana said. She was not going to miss this. The bald man's confession could be the last missing piece of the puzzle. She might finally know just exactly what happened to the Sky Walk and why.

"I don't think—"

"If you can go with that hole in your side, I can. Mine is just a 'little scratch.'"

Dawson shot her a glare. "The nurse said you should take it easy for a few days."

"Oh, yeah? Well, she said you were going against medical advice."

"Jules, you've been through a lot."

"And you haven't?" Juliana rubbed her head. "I barely remember what happened. Did I bite somebody?"

He smiled. "You bit Baldy—Schumer. You were hanging on to his belt. You did good."

"Whatever he gave me, every bit of that seems like a dream. Was I really way up above the casino?"

"Yeah. It's probably better if you don't remember it. So I'll put you to bed and then—"

"I have to give a statement anyway. I can do that while I'm there."

He sent her a disgusted glance but he didn't argue. He turned toward the Waveland police station.

When they got there, Detective Hardy greeted them. He peered at the strip bandage on her temple. "Juliana, I wasn't expecting to see you for a day or two. It looks like you're doing pretty good."

"Thank you. Where's the bald man?"

Hardy looked at Dawson, who shrugged. She chose to ignore them. "He's in the interrogation room with his lawyer. The assistant district attorney, Maura Presley, just left. She's giving him a few minutes to talk with his lawyer about her offer of a deal."

"What did she offer him?" Dawson asked.

"Well, I told her what we have on him—aggravated assault on Juliana."

"Assault? Don't you mean *attempted murder?* He was going to throw her fifty feet to the casino floor. He took her up there to murder her."

Juliana knew that—in her head, but hearing Dawson say it sent icy fear up her spine. The memory of being fifty feet above the casino on a maze of two-foot-wide beams was unreal. It seemed like a nightmare.

Hardy looked exasperated. "I thought you were the one who wanted a super-deal for him, so he'd talk."

Dawson's jaw flexed. "So what is Maura offering him?"

"Ten years—eight suspended, plus two years of supervised probation, if he testifies against Vega."

"Vega? He's going to testify against Vega? That's what the deal is for?" Juliana asked. Her heart fluttered like a panicked butterfly. Was Vega finally going to be exposed for what he really was? Then a memory that had gotten buried under the terror of her ordeal surfaced.

"Vega!" She grabbed Dawson's arm. "Dawson, I think

Vega was targeting my dad! It was something to do with his son."

Dawson nodded and jerked a thumb toward Hardy. "I've already told Brian. Your dad gave Anthony Vega a job at the Beachview Casino in Gulfport, but before long he found out Anthony was shaking down customers. Your dad had him arrested and despite Tito's influence, Anthony went to prison and was killed."

Juliana broken in. "I knew it! I knew there had to be a connection. So he blamed my dad for his son's death? That proves it, doesn't it?"

"Listen, Juliana," Detective Hardy said. "Even if we could prove that the Sky Walk was brought down deliberately at a specific time when your father was in his office, linking it to Tito Vega will be a crapshoot at best. He has friends in places so high you need an air mask. Plus, he could drag a lot of prominent people down with him—politicians, businessmen, community leaders. It's liable to be a bloodbath."

"He murdered my father. What are you saying? That you can't do it? Or that you won't?"

# Chapter Nineteen

Hardy ran a hand down his face. "We can't prove it. Our best bet is sitting right in there." He nodded toward the interrogation room. "But right now we're at a standoff. Schumer won't share what he's got until he has a deal and Maura won't offer a deal until she knows what she has to work with." Hardy gestured with his head. "There's Maura." He motioned her over.

"Maura Presley, this is Juliana Caprese and Dawson Delancey."

Maura was a tall blonde whose black-rimmed glasses couldn't hide her beauty. She was dressed conservatively, in a black suit with a no-nonsense white shirt. Her briefcase was Coach and her pumps were Alexander McQueen. She held out her hand to Juliana and then to Dawson.

"So are you about to go back in?" Hardy asked her.

"We've taken it this far. Let's go see what Schumer has to say."

"Maura, before you go in, I've got something on Vega," Dawson said. "Or I will have by early in the morning. It just might link Vega with money laundering, maybe even worse."

Maura Presley eyed him narrowly. "Might?" She sounded interested but skeptical.

He nodded. "That's why I want to hear what Schumer's got."

The three of them slipped into the viewing room as Maura

entered the interrogation room. The big bald goon sat at the table. His shirt was wrinkled and the right elbow was soaked in blood. His mouth no longer curled up in a sneer. Maura walked in, set the tape recorder on the table and flipped the switch. Schumer wiped a beefy hand down his face.

"Well, Mr. Schumer, have you had a chance to think about my offer?"

He regarded her silently and a ghost of the sneer briefly crossed his face. "What I've got is good enough to put Vega away. But if he knows that I have done this, I will not survive two months, much less two years behind bars. His fingers reach far."

Hardy whistled and Dawson slammed a fist into his palm.

"What?" Juliana asked.

"He's never mentioned Vega's name before," Hardy said, glancing at Dawson. "This could work."

Maura sat back and folded her arms. "I can put you into a maximum security federal facility in another state, *if* what you have is good enough—"

"It is!"

Maura held up her hand. "*If* it's good enough to stick," she emphasized. "If Vega walks, you go to the Mississippi State Penitentiary."

Schumer's face blanched. "I won't last a day at Parchman. Vega can snap his fingers and have me killed."

"Then you'd better hope your information is good."

The bald man nodded. "I swear it is."

Juliana touched Hardy's arm. "Do you know what he's got?"

Hardy exchanged another look with Dawson. "Let's get out of here."

He led them out of the viewing room and to his desk. He sat behind it. Dawson gestured to her to sit in the single straight-backed chair, and he stood behind her.

Hardy said, "We informed Schumer that Maynard copped to stealing the letter and that he told us Schumer had it. Schumer finally admitted it. He claims it was written by Randall Knoblock and that Knoblock enclosed a flash drive that held a recording of a telephone conversation he had with Vega."

"Of course! That was the rectangular object I felt in the envelope," Juliana said.

"Did he say what the phone conversation was?" Dawson asked.

"He said it proves Vega was the one who ordered the changes in the Sky Walk. Said Knoblock told Vega he was done with him."

"What about Knoblock. Can we find him? Will he testify?" Dawson asked.

Brian shook his head. "I've had a man checking on him. Knoblock's dead. He was killed in a car crash—hit-and-run—about a week after the letter was stolen."

"That's what my dad was afraid of. He told me Vega would never leave a loose end like Knoblock alive," Dawson said.

"Vega killed him," Juliana gasped.

"I doubt we can prove that," Brian said.

"So what about the letter and the flash drive?" Dawson continued.

"If Maura can talk Schumer into taking her deal, he'll produce the evidence. She'll have to decide if it's substantial enough, If it is, she'll send Schumer to the facility she mentioned, and take the evidence to the grand jury. This is going to be a long process at best. And I doubt seriously there's a judge in the country who will remand Vega."

"So Jules could still be in danger."

"Vega will be under a microscope once all this comes out. My guess is that with you to protect her, Juliana will be safe as houses."

She felt Dawson stiffen beside her and she knew exactly what he was thinking. After the way she'd acted when she'd seen Michael Delancey's name in his phone, he wanted nothing more than to be rid of her.

A WEEK LATER Juliana stood in the living room of her father's house and waved goodbye to a real-estate agent. The woman had given her the name of a handyman to replace the picture window and rip out the carpet. She needed to have the whole house professionally cleaned to get rid of the odors of smoke and gasoline before she had new carpet and drapes installed.

The agent had suggested that she update the kitchen with new appliances and new cabinets. Juliana told her that if she were keeping the house, she'd do a total kitchen remodel, but because she was selling it, she'd just throw in an appliance allowance for the buyers.

She felt good about the asking price. A wistful pang brought sudden tears to her eyes. She loved this house and would love to live here, but it wasn't practical. It was much too big for a single woman, and selling it would secure her future.

Several years ago, when he decided to retire, her dad had added the den and made the carport into a combination media and craft room where he tied fishing flies and tinkered with small wood projects. Then he'd added a two-car garage. Altogether, he'd increased the size of the house from 2,100 to 3,200 square feet.

She swallowed against a lump in her throat. She'd give every last penny to have her dad back. But at least Vega would pay for his part in her dad's death.

*Don't get your hopes too high,* Dawson had warned her. *If Vega draws a judge who owes him or one he's got dirt on, things might not go your way. One big thing in our favor, though, is that bank records from the Cayman Islands prove that Vega may have been laundering money through his various corporations for years.*

*Our favor.* The only reason he'd said that was because the evidence not only connected Vega with the Sky Walk, but it also helped to prove his dad wasn't responsible for the collapse.

"Get out of my head, Dawson," she muttered as she picked up the real-estate agent's card and headed for the kitchen to stick it in her purse.

"Somebody taking my name in vain?" a familiar sexy-assin voice said.

Juliana whirled. Dawson was standing in the doorway, looking like everything she'd ever dreamed of. He had on creased khaki pants and a crisp white shirt with the sleeves rolled up.

She frowned, reminding herself that he was done with her. "What are you doing here?"

He stepped inside and frowned back at her. "Was that a real-estate agent's car I saw leaving?"

She nodded. "I'm going to sell it, after I get the repairs done."

"Hmm."

"What?"

"Nothing," Dawson replied, looking around the living room. "The damage isn't too bad in here."

What was he doing here, acting all normal? "Do you have news about Vega?" she asked.

He walked over to the hall door and checked out the hall. Then he turned back to her. "Hardy told me what Knoblock's letter said. He claimed Vega ordered him to use materials that would guarantee the Sky Walk would collapse."

She tried to process that. "I don't understand. I mean, I'm glad if it's enough to put Vega away, but why would he do something that would kill innocent people?"

"Remember I told you that your dad had made notes in his day planner about Vega's son? He told your dad he'd been a friend of yours in school. Once your dad figured out that Anthony was blackmailing wealthy gamblers who were running around on their wives or cheating or whatever else he could dig up on them, your dad called the police. Anthony was arrested for extortion and blackmail."

Juliana nodded. "You gave the day planners to the assistant district attorney."

"Vega had already begun plans to build the Golden Galaxy. He was going to give it to Anthony to run. But then Anthony was killed. Vega was devastated by the death of his only son, but he went ahead with his plans to have the casino built."

"So he hired Daddy to manage it—"

"Because he blamed him for Anthony's death. It was your dad who'd put Anthony in prison. Vega wanted your dad ruined. The Sky Walk would collapse. Vega would make sure your dad never worked again. He probably didn't plan to kill him. Who knows if he thought innocent people would die. But he made sure the Sky Walk would break. It was his idea of vengeance."

"All that for vengeance against my father."

"That's the way Knoblock outlined it in his letter. The recorded phone conversation, plus my dad's testimony, should clinch it."

"Your dad?"

"My dad overheard that same telephone conversation with Knoblock. He had no idea what it meant because he only heard Knoblock's side of it. His statement to the police is almost word for word what Knoblock said on the phone."

Juliana squeezed her eyes shut. "I think I'm still very confused."

"Hey, you're the one who got all this started by figuring

out the connections between Vega and all those corporations. Because of your flowchart, I sent an investigator to Switzerland to check out Bayside Industries. What he brought back was solid gold—a connection between Bayside Industries and Meadow Gold and a bank in the Caymans. It was your research, your flowchart, that will convict Vega of money laundering."

"So Vega is facing money laundering charges? What else?"

"Probably reckless endangerment is the most they can get him on for the Sky Walk's collapse. But he's also being investigated for extortion and possible murder charges, if anything comes of Knoblock's death."

Juliana felt overwhelmed. "I don't know if I'm glad he's going to be punished or furious that he won't be serving consecutive life sentences for six murders."

"Hey," Dawson said, reaching out an arm toward her, but then hesitating. "In all these years nobody has been able to bring Vega down. You did it."

"Not by myself. And I don't really feel triumphant. Just sad."

He nodded, then turned back toward the hall door. "What's through here?" he asked, walking into the hall and across to the den. "Wow, nice den. It would make a great office."

"Haven't you seen it before?"

"No, I never made it inside the house." He turned and gave her a small smile. "I'd like to say I rescued you from the fire, but a fireman was bringing you out by the time I got here." He went to the next door off the hall.

"What's through there?" He headed toward it without waiting for her to answer.

"Dawson," she started, but he was through the door and turning on the light. She had no choice but to follow.

"What a cool room. Big-screen TV, surround sound. Why're you selling? You ought to move back here." He looked around. "A refrigerator. Your dad sure knew how to live." As soon as the words left his mouth, he grimaced. "Sorry."

She smiled. "It's okay," she said, and realized it really was. "He did know how to live. He loved football and basketball. I was stunned when he added all this, but he told me he was—" She had to stop. That lump was back. She swallowed, then continued. "He said he wanted plenty of room for—for grand-kids."

Dawson had his arms around her before she was aware that he'd moved. She stiffened. She couldn't bear to have him hold her and then walk away.

He obviously felt her go still because he let go of her, but not before planting a gentle kiss on her forehead. "I'm sorry, Jules. I know you miss him."

"So you came here to tell me about Vega? I'm glad he's going to pay for what he did. But—" she gestured vaguely in the direction of the living room "—I was just about to leave."

He took a step backward and an odd expression crossed his face. "Okay," he said. "The only other thing I have is infor-mation from Maura Presley. She's arranged for a civil lawyer to prepare briefs for a civil case against Vega, for reparations to the families of the people who died in the Sky Walk's col-lapse. She's also asked him to look into restoring my dad's architectural license."

"I'm glad, about all of it. So you and your dad—"

Dawson didn't speak for a minute. He walked over to the TV and examined it. "Yeah, we're doing okay. I realized I never gave him a chance."

Juliana looked at him. It obviously had been a big step for him to go to his dad and apologize. It had taken a lot of cour-age. Speaking of courage, if she was ever going to apologize to him, now was the time. She was afraid that once he walked out the front door she might never see him again.

She took a long breath. "I know what you mean," she said.

Dawson cocked an eyebrow at her. "What I mean about what?"

"About giving people a chance. I realized—" She'd used up all her breath, or maybe it was the tightness in her throat. She tried again. "I never gave you a chance."

He leaned against a dark wood bookcase and picked up a DVD, examining it. "Tell me more," he said without looking up.

She frowned at him. Was he mocking her? She couldn't be sure. "I should have let you explain when I—when I found out who you were—are."

"Yeah—" He took a deep breath. "I guess I should have told you who I am from the beginning."

"I understand why you didn't," she replied.

"You do?" he asked, lifting his head slightly. The odd, pensive look was still in his expression.

She nodded. "I probably would have shot you."

He nodded, but he didn't smile at her joke.

She swallowed hard. "Dawson, I want you to have—" She stopped. What had she done with it? She patted her pockets. It had been in these jeans—which she'd washed.

*Oh, please, please don't be lost.* She slid her fingers into the left front pocket and felt around.

There. Thank God. She slid her hand out and closed her fist around it. Her breath whooshed out in relief.

"What are you doing?"

"You know how many times I asked you not to call me Jules?"

He nodded, looking wary. "A lot."

"Well, it was because that's what my dad called me. I didn't want anyone else—I didn't want you—that close."

He looked down at the DVD.

"Here," she said, stepping closer to him. She was going

to chicken out if she didn't get it over with. "Hold out your hand."

He did, frowning.

"I want you to have this. It was my dad's. It was very special to him. He'd have liked you. He'd have—told me to get over myself." She ran the words together, afraid she might cry before she got them out.

She had no idea what he would do—she had no idea what she wanted him to do. All she knew was that for whatever reason, it seemed right that he should have her dad's wedding ring. It was little enough payment for everything he'd done for her.

"What is this?" He held it up, then brought it closer and squinted. "Do you know what's engraved on here?"

She nodded. *Here they came.* The tears. She sniffed and wiped her eyes. "I know. My mom did it. She had it engraved and gave it to Daddy on their wedding day."

He looked stunned. "What am I supposed to do with it?" he asked, his voice sounding hoarse.

"I—I don't know. Wear it? Put it in a box somewhere?" She wiped the tears away and stuck her chin out. "Pawn it if things get tough?"

His throat moved as he swallowed. He frowned, raised his brows, frowned again. Then he laughed.

"Don't—" she started, but he held up a hand.

"No, wait—" he gasped. "You're not going to believe this."

Juliana's heart wrenched, hurt by his laughter.

But the laughter stopped and he grew solemn. He drew in a long breath. "I was talking to my mom and dad last night and, well, you came up. I was telling them about your wanting to be a private investigator and how—" he cleared his throat "—how brave and determined you are."

He stopped, twirling her dad's ring on the tip of his index

finger and staring at it. "Mom, she's brave and determined, too. You'll like her."

Juliana was speechless. She'd never seen Dawson like this. He was awkward, maybe even shy.

"So my mom gives me a look and goes to her room and comes back with something. She—you'd have to know her—" he said, shaking his head. "She still treats me like I'm sixteen. She patted my cheek and said maybe it was time she gave it to me." He sucked in a breath, as if his words had used up all his air.

"Gave what to you?" Juliana's lungs felt deflated, too. She didn't dare to guess what he was talking about.

He reached into his back pocket and pulled something out—a box. Tiny. Velvet.

"Wh-what's that?" she asked, hardly able to hear herself over the pounding of her heart.

He fumbled with it for a second, then finally opened it. Inside, on a black velvet pillow, was the most beautiful ring she had ever seen. The gold setting mimicked flower petals and on each petal was a diamond or a ruby.

"Oh," she said, choking on the word. "What—what is that? Why are you showing it to me?"

"Because my mom told me to."

Her gaze snapped to his. "What?"

He smiled. "I think I already knew, but I can be a little dense sometimes. My mom told me to tell you that I love you."

"You—"

He nodded. "This was my grandmother's ring, and I'd be most honored if you'd consider wearing it. I'd like for us to be partners."

"Partners? Dawson, I don't understand what you're talking about. The ring, it's too much. It's—"

He grinned at her. "I need somebody who's as good at

paperwork and research as you are because I hate that stuff. I want you to come to work for me, as my partner."

"Your partner." Something didn't sound right. He was holding a beautiful, priceless ring and talking about *hiring* her.

"Yeah. In D&D Services. But we'll have to change that."

"Change what?" She felt like a parrot. All she could do was repeat what he said.

"The name. Not change it exactly. Just its meaning. It was Dedicated and Discreet. Now it'll be Delancey and Delancey."

"Delancey and—"

Dawson picked up her hand and slipped the ring onto her left ring finger. "And Delancey." Then he looked up at her with what looked like fear in his eyes.

"Hmm," she said, frowning at him. "If you're going to be a married man, you're going to have to say what you mean."

He laughed and shook his head. "I guess I am. Will you wear my grandmother's ring and promise to never leave me?"

Juliana stared at him until his brows drew down and his intense blue eyes darkened. She realized she hadn't answered him, so she threw herself into his arms.

He kissed her. For a long time they kissed and nuzzled and whispered and kissed some more. Then Dawson lifted his head. "Does this house have any bedrooms?" he asked.

Juliana giggled and took his hand. "Yes. This way," she said and led him to her room.

"This is yours," he said.

She nodded. "But wait. I haven't said whether I'll wear your grandmother's ring." She took a deep breath. "I will—if you'll wear my dad's ring."

"I will," he said solemnly. He handed her the ring and she slipped it onto his left ring finger. "It fits perfectly," he said.

"That's because you have perfect fingers." She kissed each

one of them. Then she raised her head and kissed him. Soon both of them were breathless.

"Don't you like this house?" he asked her as he unbuttoned her shirt.

"Yes, of course I do," she answered as she unbuttoned his. "But it's too big for me."

"Sell it to me," he said, sliding her shirt down off her shoulders and kissing her skin.

"You?" Her fingers quit working. "Why?"

He kissed the curve of her shoulder and traced it up to her neck with his lips. "I've always wanted a big house, and I have a feeling we're going to need one. Just because your dad's not right here with us doesn't mean we can't fill this house with grandchildren for him."

Juliana beamed as tears filled her eyes. "No, it doesn't. Are you suggesting we get started now? Because I think that's a great idea."

\* \* \* \* \*

# SUSPENSE

**Harlequin**

# INTRIGUE

**COMING NEXT MONTH**
AVAILABLE JUNE 12, 2012

### #1353 WRANGLED
*Whitehorse, Montana: Chisholm Cattle Company*
**B.J. Daniels**

### #1354 HIGH NOON
*Colby, TX*
**Debra Webb**

### #1355 EYEWITNESS
*Guardians of Coral Cove*
**Carol Ericson**

### #1356 DEATH OF A BEAUTY QUEEN
*The Delancey Dynasty*
**Mallory Kane**

### #1357 THUNDER HORSE HERITAGE
**Elle James**

### #1358 SPY HARD
**Dana Marton**

# REQUEST YOUR FREE BOOKS!
## 2 FREE NOVELS PLUS 2 FREE GIFTS!

**Harlequin**

# INTRIGUE

### BREATHTAKING ROMANTIC SUSPENSE

**YES!** Please send me 2 FREE Harlequin Intrigue® novels and my 2 FREE gifts (gifts are worth about $10). After receiving them, if I don't wish to receive any more books, I can return the shipping statement marked "cancel." If I don't cancel, I will receive 6 brand-new novels every month and be billed just $4.49 per book in the U.S. or $5.24 per book in Canada. That's a saving of at least 14% off the cover price! It's quite a bargain! Shipping and handling is just 50¢ per book in the U.S. and 75¢ per book in Canada.* I understand that accepting the 2 free books and gifts places me under no obligation to buy anything. I can always return a shipment and cancel at any time. Even if I never buy another book, the two free books and gifts are mine to keep forever.

182/382 HDN FEQ2

Name _____ (PLEASE PRINT)

Address _____ Apt. #

City _____ State/Prov. _____ Zip/Postal Code

Signature (if under 18, a parent or guardian must sign)

Mail to the **Reader Service:**
**IN U.S.A.:** P.O. Box 1867, Buffalo, NY 14240-1867
**IN CANADA:** P.O. Box 609, Fort Erie, Ontario L2A 5X3

Not valid for current subscribers to Harlequin Intrigue books.

**Are you a subscriber to Harlequin Intrigue books
and want to receive the larger-print edition?
Call 1-800-873-8635 or visit www.ReaderService.com.**

\* Terms and prices subject to change without notice. Prices do not include applicable taxes. Sales tax applicable in N.Y. Canadian residents will be charged applicable taxes. Offer not valid in Quebec. This offer is limited to one order per household. All orders subject to credit approval. Credit or debit balances in a customer's account(s) may be offset by any other outstanding balance owed by or to the customer. Please allow 4 to 6 weeks for delivery. Offer available while quantities last.

**Your Privacy**—The Reader Service is committed to protecting your privacy. Our Privacy Policy is available online at www.ReaderService.com or upon request from the Reader Service.

We make a portion of our mailing list available to reputable third parties that offer products we believe may interest you. If you prefer that we not exchange your name with third parties, or if you wish to clarify or modify your communication preferences, please visit us at www.ReaderService.com/consumerchoice or write to us at Reader Service Preference Service, P.O. Box 9062, Buffalo, NY 14269. Include your complete name and address.

HI11B

*Harlequin® Romantic Suspense presents the final book
in the gripping* PERFECT, WYOMING *miniseries
from best-loved veteran series author Carla Cassidy*

**Witness as mercenary Micah Grayson and cult escapee
Olivia Conner join forces to save a little boy and to take
down a monster, while desire explodes between them....**

*Read on for an excerpt from*
*MERCENARY'S PERFECT MISSION*

*Available June 2012 from Harlequin® Romantic Suspense.*

"**I** won't tell," she exclaimed fervently. "Please don't hurt me. I swear I won't tell anyone what I saw. Just let me have my other son and we'll go far away from here. I'll never speak your name again." Her voice cracked as she focused on his gun and he realized she believed he was Samuel.

Certainly it was dark enough that it would be easy for anyone to mistake him for his brother. When the brothers were together it was easy to see the subtle differences between them. Micah's face was slightly thinner, his features more chiseled than those of his brother.

At the moment Micah knew Samuel kept his hair cut neat and tidy, while Micah's long hair was tied back. He reached up and pulled the rawhide strip, allowing his hair to fall from its binding.

The woman gasped once again. "You aren't him...but you look like him. Who are you?" Her voice still held fear as she dropped the stick and protectively clutched the baby closer to her chest.

"Who are you?" he countered. He wasn't about to be taken in by a pale-haired angel with big green eyes in this evil place where angels probably couldn't exist.

"I'm Olivia Conner, and this is my son Sam." Tears filled her eyes. "I have another son, but he's still in town. I couldn't get to him before I ran away. I've heard rumors that there was a safe house somewhere, but I've been in the woods for two days and I can't find it."

Micah was unmoved by her tears and by her story. He knew how devious his brother could be, and Micah would do everything possible to protect the location of the safe house. There was only one way to know for sure if she was one of Samuel's "devotees."

*Will Olivia be able to get her son back from the clutches of evil? Or will Micah's maniacal twin put an end to them all? Find out in the shocking conclusion to the* PERFECT, WYOMING *miniseries.*

*MERCENARY'S PERFECT MISSION*
*Available June 2012, only from*
*Harlequin® Romantic Suspense, wherever books are sold.*

# SPECIAL EDITION

### Life, Love and Family

*USA TODAY* bestselling author

# Marie Ferrarella

enchants readers in

## ONCE UPON A MATCHMAKER

Micah Muldare's aunt is worried that her nephew is going to wind up alone in his old age...but this matchmaking mama has just the thing! When Micah finds himself accused of theft, defense lawyer Tracy Ryan agrees to help him as a favor to his aunt, but soon finds herself drawn to more than just his case. Will Micah open up his heart and realize Tracy is his match?

### *Available June 2012*

Saddle up with Harlequin® series books this summer and find a cowboy for every mood!

*Available wherever books are sold.*

www.Harlequin.com

HSE65674

**Harlequin** *Romance*

*A touching new duet from fan-favorite author*

# SUSAN MEIER

*First Time* **DADS!**

When millionaire CEO Max Montgomery spots
Kate Hunter-Montgomery—the wife he's never forgotten—
back in town with a daughter who looks just like him, he's
determined to win her back. But can this savvy business tycoon
convince Kate to trust him a second time with her heart?

*Find out this June in*

## THE TYCOON'S SECRET DAUGHTER

*And look for book 2 coming this August!*

## NANNY FOR THE MILLIONAIRE'S TWINS

Saddle up with Harlequin® series books this summer
and find a cowboy for every mood!

HRI7811